EXISTENCE

THE DEVILGOD BOOK 1

S.C. LEWIS

WWW.FACEBOOK.COM/DevilGodBook/
TWITTER: @CSLUIS2

Special thanks to Anton LaVey

Dedicated to Anne Rice

PRELUDE

CHIEF OF THUNDER

Rain echoed loudly from the roof of the car. Sounds of shattering glass broke through the falling rain from somewhere outside in the darkness. I sat in the rear of the black Lincoln, watching rain hit the windshield and drip down the car window. It was dark and menacing outside, dark and deepening blue. Lightning flashed in the sky, and only when the light flared all around did I catch my reflection in the car's rear-view mirror.

The face of an older fellow was framed by long hair that was so blonde it was almost white. It was tied in a ponytail, and two large gray eyes stared back at me. Glimmering pale skin boldly hummed from my face. Was I that *obvious?* I smiled at myself; my pearly canines greeted me in return from beyond the curving flesh of my lips. The thin lips disappeared as I pulled my mouth back, closing it.

"Why are we here, sir?" a voice broke through the falling rain.

Only then did I gaze up from the back seat to the questioning eyes of my driver, Rufus, and fully realize I wasn't alone in this dreadful weather.

"We're waiting for someone," I stated firmly. "Someone is coming," I let a quiet sigh escape my lips.

1

He seemed satisfied with my answer. Though I sensed further questions stirring in his mind, he spoke no more. I never said much, and he never seemed to question that. He always did what he was told, with great devotion and respect. His thoughts never troubled me. He didn't fear me, though at times he found my behavior both peculiar and alarming. But never once did he challenge me.

I was a private man, who paid him very well, and never asked much from him, nor placed him in harm's way. Just like any other day, he was satisfied with my answer and sat quietly behind the wheel, waiting with me in this dreadful rain for "the someone" who was coming. The sounds of the pouring rain muffled all other things around us.

I gazed out the car window again. The streets were deserted this cold and wet evening; only the unfortunate homeless were out there, huddling for shelter within the downtown alleys. My Lincoln was parked near one of these, where only moments earlier two street people had come up to the car begging for money. I gave freely to the needy, willing to frighten those that didn't leave me be afterwards.

I watched the raindrops fall, falling myself into a rain-sodden trance. I watched as the drops suddenly turned into blood. I flinched as a golden flash of lightning brought their watery color back. I gasped, catching Rufus' eyes tracing my face from the rear-view mirror. He seemed concerned for me. I waved his feelings away, falling back into the trance, watching with amazement as the newly bloody skies fell. There was no rain anymore, only blood that fell from the sky. As promised, God wasn't flooding the world again; he was obviously badly wounded. No mere mortal could ever see that. Why did we need the blood to survive? We didn't. We had the poison, and we had the seed and the thorns. God needed the blood, but our wild and untamed fluid was too poisonous, too likely to flood the planet before God Himself ever could.

Suddenly, once again I stood at the foot of a stormy cliff, recalling everything. This time, however, Hell's oceans did not greet me, nor did the bloody sands of the beach. This was a new chapter, a new realm that I walked. I questioned whether I was its first visitor. This place was dreadfully beautiful. The sky was a gloomy shade of midnight blue. Trees that resembled twisting vines, with brightly burning green leaves on their branches, moaned in the wind. The ground could barely be seen, covered in a light mist, where beneath the haze long stems of grassy arms came up to my knees. Like the sticky stingers of honeybees, they stung my bare feet. They seemed to be drawn to me; like sucking leeches, they swayed around my legs, painfully piercing my skin with their tiny ends.

I rushed through them, escaping their bites, onto a cobblestone path. From there, I watched the landscape shaping itself; the mist made it barely visible to my eyes. Before the cliff moved, a beautiful gray-green world, with only somber gray mists surrounding it appeared. It was fantastic, laid out in bleak wonder and mysterious power.

It was warm- neither cold nor hot. The colors of the landscape were bright, brilliant greens and reds shining radiantly from the heads of the flowers. The air was sweet, with the scent of the flowers wafting through its swift currents.

As I turned, I spotted a man's form walking on the stone path towards me. He vanished. In a wink, he reappeared closer, each glance bringing him even nearer until he stood only a step from me. The silent figure was draped in a black cloak. When he lifted the hood, a beautiful young man's gray eyes stared back at me from deep within its billowing folds. His long, red hair covered his shoulders as a grin spread over his simple full lips. In a flash, a woman's face smiled from the hood instead.

Sabelle?

I jumped up as looming, rolling thunder broke my trance. Rufus was turning to me that very moment, trying hard to get my attention.

"Sir, I think someone is here." Rufus pointed towards the alley.

Dazed, I turned and gazed out of the car window through the running raindrops.

I caught sight of a form in the distance darkly approaching.

Again, a lightning flash brought a cloaked image into my eyes. I now recalled the face of the woman...

"Sabelle," I whispered to myself.

Rufus glanced in my direction, but said nothing.

Another flash in the distant sky brought me to the cliff again; the rain was no longer falling, though the sky certainly was. As I gazed up into the heavens, giant balls of fire and flames stormed down all around me. I stood again on that very same cliff, but this time in Hell, staring down at the black oceans and watching the mortals drown as they fought to escape its mile-high currents.

The sky was black, gray, painted blue, and yes, always red with the infernal flames of the grand pits.

Angels soared above me, diving into the black oceans as if searching for something. A feeling overcame me suddenly, a presence of fear and excitement bringing me to my feet as again my eyes shot into the black ocean waves in search of its special spark.

At once, a single, bright-red light shone from the ominous waves, summoning me to the crumbling edge of the sheerest of yawning cliffs as I dangerously teetered upon it; but my reborn wings dramatically extended, keeping me safe upon the ground.

By my very toes I remained gripped to the ledge! It was only then that I saw her face washing out from every wave in the blackest oceans of Hell. It *was* her! She had come back. At once I leapt into the sky, diving past several angels flying closely nearby. My skyward dash brought their gazes to my attention, and they followed me without pause or mercy. I tried to fight them off, shoving boldly at one or two of them as they flew past me. I couldn't let them get ahead of me. *This moment was mine!*

Yet they were just as determined as I was to get there first. I struggled savagely, floating in the air with one of the angels as he shoved his arm into my stomach and dove straight ahead of me. Enraged, I swiftly caught up with him, and pulled out the silver sword blade at my side. I struck him on his left wing.

All at once, he turned angrily, fiercely trying to shove me back. I recognized him, and he knew me.

"Not this time, Ramiel!" he hissed from beneath his grinding teeth. His angelical visage showed only naked rage as he bore down on me with unstoppable fury.

"She is ours!" he screamed into my face.

"I will not allow it!" I roared back in desperation.

"There is nothing you can do, traitor!" He grabbed my sword, flinging it out into the yawning abyss, which silently swallowed it. With a lurch of crazed strength, I grabbed him and tossed him over me backwards; as he fell, he crashed resoundingly into two other angels. Losing them all for a moment, I flew quickly through the skies and over the black ocean waters in search of my only hope, my one lasting light. A glimmer of red in the ocean alerted me, and I dove into the waters, reaching through the icy liquid.

I extended both arms deeply into the crashing black waters, in search of her. A red mass of seaweed- like hair, or like cobwebs-draped over my flailing hands as I desperately hovered just above the pounding, cold seas.

All at once, a frozen, naked arm shot out from the waves, grasping mine. I pulled the lost soul out. Her web of scarlet hair scattered water as it draped across her face. I could clearly see it was her. She trembled, but her eyes remained closed. Her open lips shuddered, and were blue in color. She had been under for a very long time. The icy oceans of Hell had consumed her fragile body. I could feel her gasping for breath as she collapsed within my closing arms. Straining upwards, pounding my wings, I lifted her from the hideous waters into the air with me, triumphantly embracing her tightly. She was *alive!*

She came awake in my throbbing, painful arms, wrapping hers tightly around my straining neck. She kissed my chin, dropping her weary head upon my heaving chest as we slowly mounted into the ruby skies. I placed my large hand over her dripping, cold head, allowing my warmth to permeate her freezing skin. Soon, she stopped trembling, and a grateful sigh escaped her lips.

"Thank you, Ramiel," she whispered through her beautifully small mouth, never opening her eyes. Again, she collapsed, hanging limp in my equally grateful embrace.

My moments alone with her were short-lived. Above my wearied wings, the rest of the angels were swiftly approaching. A band of them flew ahead, coming towards us. Immediately, I swooped into the sky with her draped over my arms; the angels followed us with a most dreadful speed. They were determined to wrestle her from me!

I flew over the majestically beautiful but unspeakably infinite landscapes of Hell. Behind me, the angels closely pursued. If I could make it to the swirling gates at the other end of this realm, we would be away from this awful place, and my Sabelle would be safe at last.

I flew in between the dead trees, narrowly skirting their branches, avoiding the clutching arms that were widely outspread, reaching and trying to take hold of us. Suddenly, two angels appeared beside us, gripping my arms in an attempt to slow us down. I shoved both elbows back with my greatest strength, and successfully released myself from their embrace.

Another one swung a gleaming sword blade at my side, barely missing me. I rose high up into the sky, tearing away from the clutching trees, but the ever-present angels always followed. I kicked one or two off of us, but there were too many; it seemed the whole angelical realm had gathered to stop me and to steal my Sabelle away.

I heard shouts from a distance as others approached to aid the seemingly demoniacal angels surrounding us. But once again, the strange feelings overcame me, and Sabelle stirred in my arms as if she were calling on other forces to come to our aid, or maybe she was merely dreaming, oblivious to our present nightmarish danger. She kissed my neck gently as her tiny lips whispered something I couldn't make out.

A glowing light above us caught my attention, and I gazed up as the strange feelings of excitement overwhelmed both the other angels and me. From out of the light, a form slowly descended, dropping right before us. Although distracted by the light, the fearsome angels finally pinned me, trapping my wings, fighting me for ownership of Sabelle. An angel lifted his sharp blade to my weary face, but then a glowing hand reached out and quietly stopped him.

When I looked upon his face, he who had blocked the blow was staring straight at me. Esphen's smile warmly greeted me. He, being no coward, would more than ably help us all.

Esphen lightly tossed the angel away; lifting his sword, he challenged the others with the same unequivocal courage. He advanced, with his mighty blade pointed bluntly and threateningly at the entire surprised angelic host.

Slowly, these hideous demons backed off, though remaining watchful of us, too frightened of Esphen to approach.

"Go and do what you have to, Demon! *Leave this place!*" he shouted through his trumpeting mouth. A grotesquely sinister smile flashed across his beautiful face.

He joyfully lifted the sword; its light glaring at the angels in front, as beside him another form swiftly materialized. As I stared in lost stupefaction, I saw it was Gabriel who happily flew beside me, briefly protecting us. He pointed ahead to the swirl in the sky, achingly just within reach in the almost closeable distance.

"Go, Demon! Get away!" he shouted, also drawing his sword blade and wielding it mightily. The angels behind us called out to me in rank despair, trying vainly to convince me...otherwise.

"Ramiel, remember what you truly are! Ramiel, *give her to us!*"

"Pay no attention to them. Go!" Esphen snapped, taking a sharp blow to his side from a gloatingly confident angry angel. He bled; scarlet ribbons of blood which whipped rapidly through the red blowing wind as he valiantly fought back. They were both so hopelessly outnumbered.

Esphen turned and stared straight at me, and in his eyes, I clearly saw the red-haired Princess, all the poison and the inescapable web the dragon weaves, the lies and what would become of everyone if this were to last any longer. I began to weep, afraid of feelings I couldn't control, terrified of what I couldn't stop, horrified of who I was.

But with the last ounce of my vast demoniacal strength, I immediately broke free, mounting to the light above in the sky. It was then the desperate battle behind us began. The enemy angels, frightened as they were but determined, jumped through the red-stained skies to get past Esphen and Gabriel.

But Esphen was too quick for them. He swung his sword doughtily, neatly slicing off the heads of two approaching angels. Gabriel lifted his shining blade in the same manner, driving its pointed end repeatedly into the sides of his brother angels, knocking them down into the black seas below.

A flash of lightning shook me out of my trance. I realized I stood outside of the car, a short distance from glaring lights in the alley flooding into the darkness.

Rufus stood stoically behind me, holding the black umbrella over my head. I took a hesitant step into the alley, the weird excitement racing throughout my entire body. Raw smells of waste filled the air, but that was not what made me cringe, though I couldn't say the same for Rufus, who was forced to cover his nose with his white pocket-handkerchief. Death was quite near, and its taste and smell deeply stirred my vitals, like it always did.

Again, the terrible thunder roared over us, nearly knocking poor Rufus off his feet. As I moved closer to the sickening light, I ignored his singular kindness of covering me with the umbrella, walking far ahead of him as he stumbled manfully behind.

Inside the alley, a lonely form staggered free, and almost seemed to materialize from the nowhere before us. From past experience, I knew that wasn't far from the truth. The peculiar feelings overpowered me; the lightning seemed to strike right behind me, as I stood transfixed, swaying under its power and guidance. Presently, eerie light hummed out from my whitish blonde hair, and I could feel it inside my immortal body, changing me.

I was more than alive for at least this moment, and now there was nothing to fear but my own failure. In a flash, the light left me, and again, I caught sight of the figure staggering ever closer. Rufus stood over me, shakily holding out the umbrella.

"Wait here for me," I ordered. The raindrops soaked my white hair, running down my pale face as I left Rufus behind; they brushed against my thin lips. I could playfully taste them on the tip of my tongue, and they ran down my eyes, vastly refreshing me.

Rufus obeyed as usual, though I could tell he was very frightened for me. Easing his mind with a gentle gesture, I stepped forward, walking unafraid into the darkness to meet the unknown figure of my visitor. I was a part of this now; no matter what happened next, I was a most definite and integral participant. As should be the case, and that *is* how I always want things.

The shadowy figure faced me down, a mere step away. Light danced all around its face, yet I couldn't see any noticeable features. I couldn't meet its eyes; I could, however, see wet hair draping an almost familiar face. Lightning flashed again in the blood-red sky, crashing down on us, bringing Rufus and me almost to our knees.

Stumbling backwards, I turned to glance at Rufus shivering from beneath the umbrella. Waving him away, I turned to face the form in front of me. The figure swirled dizzyingly before me; suddenly something seemed to possess its form as it took on a definite identity. He, or whatever he was, stumbled forward slightly, then balanced himself, the lightning above us rang with its furious demands, but I had already been rooted to the spot by the commanding visitor, and had lost all interest in the reverberating world around me.

Within the lightning, and in one startled glimpse of everything-the roaring thunder, the fear surrounding us, the awful stench and the sound of the raindrops blasting the concrete pavement, a million times louder, echoing and vibrating- I abruptly transitioned into total attention and life.

Taut anticipation was in the air, and was so completely real. It was as realistic as the thunder and lightning, as intense as the rain and wind that blew across my cold, wet face.

A sighing breath escaped the peculiar figure; then, the lightning finally displayed its face for me. For a moment I saw the blackest and most beautiful eyes I have ever seen.

A more wonderful feeling than ever before overcame me, and emotion seemed to creep from every fiber of my being. Soft, milky skin like a cloud coalescing in the heavens, eyes like the dark sky filled with millions of vibrating stars, and those lips like rose petals! In the flashes of light above us, petals were falling instead of raindrops, and in my hands, I was suddenly holding a fragrant black rose, the thorns slicing deeply into my wetly outstretched palms.

Yet no sweet blood was dripping from my wounded hands, the blackness having eaten away the red color of the rose's petals, and deepest poison fully possessed the rose and me, digging into my soul like a teeming crowd of leering faces...lurching forwards...death.

"No!" I gasped, stumbling back, but this latest illusion had faded, and before me was an angelic figure, his face no longer hidden in the shadows, all his obscured shape no longer unfamiliar. I was looking at Him!

"Sarvakk!" I shrieked in a voice too choked for words. Why was I blessed with this honor and this curse, all in one? It was the moment a million dread, a horror a million would rather not face, but here I was before the Awareness Itself, looking deeply into His eyes, breathing the air that He breathed, if He could also breathe like me. Yes! Of course, It could, It was the Awareness, It could do anything and everything It wanted.

This was the true Awareness, which no one knew; no one could ever fathom, or understand how it had begun. And here It was standing before me; as yet again I sobbed.

The Awareness, that had both guided and tempted Christ Himself, the One whom had written the original Scriptures, the One whom had been the puppeteer, so to speak, of the events of this world. And the Awareness was now here, this very minute, standing before me, delivering Himself to the world once again, like a dying savior.

Lightning struck the sky furiously once again, the thunder immediately following, angrily hungering for my attention. I glanced at it but slightly; turning again as lightning lit the alley. The Man that I had once seen was gone; the heavenly face and the dark eyes that had consumed me had become the eyes of some other, even more beautiful creature.

The figure staggered, her legs wobbling, and then collapsed into my waiting arms. I embraced her tightly, my hands still shaking as I caressed the moist red web of hair. I laid my hand on her small head, stroking its clinging strands like they were grains of precious gold, but then the strands were as black as the oceans of Hell, and I knew just like before, the ultimate poison had possessed the rose, and now the poison possessed her.

Rufus immediately dropped the umbrella, rushing to my side to help. I lifted the girl in my rain-soaked arms, carrying her over to the Lincoln. Rufus followed, confusion stirring inside him, questions with no answers disturbing his mind. I said nothing; always his thoughts questioned me, but never did his lips move to seek any answers.

Her eyes were closed, and from her lips a single breath escaped as she nuzzled near me for warmth, just as she had before in the freezing currents of that blackened hellish sea, whereas one winged being, and as the Demon, I had first embraced her.

"Ramiel," I heard her whisper softly before she collapsed silently into my arms.

God, here she was. She was with me in Reality at last, the Holiest Grail of the universe, the blessed answer to every single blasted question anyone has ever had.

Rufus gathered his umbrella, and opened the door for me. I carefully tucked the girl under a blanket on the back seat of the Lincoln, covering her gently and well.

"Where to, Mr. DeStefano?" Rufus asked, glancing back at me

from the rear-view mirror as he took the driver's seat. "Home please, Rufus."

"And the lady, sir?"

"The lady shall be joining us, Rufus," I gruffly answered, glaring into the mirror at him.

"If you don't mind me saying, sir. The poor thing looks half-starved, doesn't she?"

"I shall nurse her back to health."

"That's very nice of you, sir. Helping a complete stranger."

I grinned; my canines barely revealed in the darkness of the vehicle.

"Whoever said she was a stranger, Rufus?"

Rufus coughed, having gotten awfully wet in the downpour, barely glancing back before he fell into utmost silence again. He drove us home without another word.

I
Houston, Texas
Thoughts

Sitting on the couch,
With nothing to do.
I wonder what everyone else is up to?
I wonder if one day
Pigs could fly?
I think by then
I probably will die.
I wonder how to make a quilt,
I think this chair is starting to tilt.
I wonder about the shoes I wear.
I think I should brush my hair.
I wonder if tomorrow I'll see that boy,
I think I want to play with a toy.
I wonder how the little fan works.
I think about eating with forks.
Sitting on the couch with tons to think,
I wonder if the toilet stinks.

BY MICHELLE PEREZ

1

MR. ABUDA

ERIC

I wasn't looking forward to speaking with Mr. Abuda this evening. As a matter of fact, he kind of scared me just a little. Why was I so unfortunate? The fact that he had called me to his office simply made me nervous. My hands were trembling as I ascended the grand staircase that led to the office. I could see the door of the office open wide just as I reached the top. I could imagine his form sitting on his mother's old leather office chair, and that made me cringe just a tiny bit.

My steps echoed as I came to the level where the office sat, dividing the dancing-dome floor on the opposite side of the arches, below where the antechamber and the foyer connected.

I didn't hear any sounds coming from inside the office, but I knew that he was in there working on business deals and other offers from clients that had come to meet with him earlier.

My hands were shaking as I came closer. They always did whenever I met with him. I could feel my heart pounding within my chest and the blood in my veins racing. Why was I so scared of him? I had never been before. In fact, I could still remember the day his mother had announced she was pregnant with him. The look on her face, the words soaring from her lips with delight and excitement as she jumped from her seat and spoke so suddenly. It seemed to be an announcement I didn't regard with the greatest of wonder, until now.

"I have something to tell you..."

Sophia's large, brown, sparkling eyes were lit so beautifully by the florescent lamps above us, and so they were caught magically in her pupils. She was dressed in a long, red, satin dress, her dark hair came down over her shoulders. She was the most beautiful thing I had ever laid eyes on.

"What is it, Sophia?" We all looked over at her, our red lips dropped in utter shock with the anticipation of her news.

My companions tried to find an answer among each other, but there was nothing but confusion surrounding the table.

"I'm pregnant," came her announcement so simple it gave no room for anything else. It was just that simple.

I rose first from my seat near the table, where all the others were glaring back at her with wide eyes. I looked at her with a single questioning stare.

If only Ramiel were here, the thought crossed my mind suddenly, for apparently no reason. It seemed that only with our boss could things continue, or be resolved without trouble...

Sophia smiled at all of us, but soon after, her eyes begged for a word from us.

"Well, isn't anybody going to say anything?" she asked regarding our silence.

The others remained confused, doubting the truth to those words.

"Sophia, that's wonderful!" Damien suddenly rose from her seat to say this, breaking the long silence. She moved over to Sophia and embraced her, kissing her gently on the cheek.

I didn't move; frozen by a strange feeling, I remained on the spot.

The others took their turns wishing Sophia congratulations with warm kisses and loving embraces. Santiago and Valentino soon took their turns hugging Sophia as well.

Santiago hesitated at first, being the flirt that he was with Sophia. He bowed, smiling and baring the long double canines behind his painted red mouth. His white ghostly face glimmered, while beyond his penetrating sharp green eyes flashed and sparkled over at her in lustful longing, an obvious crush we had grown tired of over the years. Sophia was well aware of it.

"My dear, my heart is broken. I no less adore you." He grinned and kissed the back of her hand, hoping perhaps that his vampiric charms would work on her as it had on many foolish others.

"Santiago!" I called out simply to catch his attention.

I came from behind and put a hand on his shoulder, hoping to save Sophia the embarrassment of Santiago's sometimes outrageous behavior. We neared one another. He turned and glared directly at me, his rival here again to ruin his chances at anything; perhaps these were his thoughts.

He gazed back at Sophia, "Forgive me...Where are my manners?"

He stepped aside, wandering from the others to the opposite end of the room. Santiago was always like that, withdrawn even from his own crowd, a loner, even in his own world. He dressed in a long dark coat, with a black top hat, a vest and trousers and a cane which he sometimes used to conjure his own magically generated roses. Think of it as a sort of pick-up line. Whenever the task was needed to entice a beauty, the cane was used.

Sophia smiled and held herself from saying anything as she watched Santiago wander away. Her eyes shifted to the windows of her small office glancing out the glass to the giant dance floor.

I followed her eyes, watching her stray from me to where Santiago stood. Santiago knew she was staring after him, and for that reason he barely glanced back over his shoulder towards her. Perhaps she worried about him. I knew that could be the only reason she stared after him. For she was that kind-hearted.

"Sophia, I'm so happy for you and Nathan. I can't believe it. It's such wonderful news!"

The others came closer. Damien and Damon as well as Angelo,

whose long, white mane made him appear like a banshee. Even our newer member Riccardo, a seventeen-year-old runaway, had found his display most exciting. Riccardo had joined the coven over the weekend. Damien brought home all sorts of strays, and this time it hadn't been a dog.

Valentino was near the window by Santiago's side; for some reason or another they had always been closer to each other than the others.

I glanced back at them wondering why they chose to separate themselves from those that were like them. They, without a doubt, loved Sophia, but no matter what, they did what they wanted. I knew they would never go against Sophia's words; they'd rather question my authority whenever the chance came. I had no power over their actions, and only by Sophia's wishes did they ever do anything when I said it.

Valentino frowned back at me, growling beneath his breath. He dressed in the same eighteenth-century apparel as Santiago, with the long black tailcoat and the vest in a lovely emerald color. A long collar covered his neck and was decorated with a claw pendant. Valentino's face was painted in the same manner, to give him the pale appearance of a real vampire. Only when I looked at them did I realize how much they reminded me of Lestat and Louis, from *Interview with the Vampire*. That book was a bible to us and real enough.

We referred to them as the Elders, because they were older than any of us, and far wiser in the vampiric sense of the word. Older in human reality, and just as old in vampire reality, which only meant they had done this most of their lives. They resembled eighteenth-century European vampires, with the silk top hat, the long dark cape, jacket, vest and walking cane. They had seen the worst of days, and the grayest of nights. They'd partaken in blood rituals of all sorts- humans as well as animals- or so they liked to tell people. I knew nothing but what the others knew, what they told others.

We respected them because they were older Goth. Like human parents, the Elders were our guidance. A dying breed, instinctively abandoned by everyone, including their own children. These were the vampire rules we knew, in our lovely and long-lost Vampire Reality. This was the vampire reality we followed.

Santiago was a savage in his feeding, sometimes biting and leaving teeth markings on his companions. It had not be a secret that he fancied doing the same one day to Sophia. To drink her blood would surely satisfy him greatly.

That was his fantasy; I wouldn't have known if he hadn't written it into his journal, which I happened to come across. In the other pages were his many names and descriptions of all of us.

As for Valentino, he cared for Santiago in ways I believe Santiago might have not been aware. I knew his sexual orientation and he preferred both. He also had his eyes on Sophia, but he would let Santiago have her if it meant he could win his heart.

Valentino stared at me; his face fell forward vengefully. His hazel eyes penetrated and could cut the air around us. His vacant, hollow expression housed a warning. The *vampire stare*, the grimace that meant death. An expression most vamps gave their victims, but for vampires it meant, *I don't like you.*

"Oh, it's so wonderful!" Damien cried delightfully. "I wonder what it's going to be? When's your due date, Sophie? Did you tell Nathan, yet? Oh, this is so *exciting!*"

The others seemed as delighted as she did. Riccardo and Angelo were jumping up and down along with Damien thinking of all the things they must prepare for the moment of triumph. They just loved that. It meant "gold and riches" to them, an immortal something that couldn't ever be abandoned.

"Well, the doctor said I'm due in October. Nathan knows. Anyway, we talked about it. And we both thought it was about time we started having a family."

"Oh, this is the best news I've heard all day!" Damien exclaimed, holding unto Sophia's arm.

"We have to throw Sophie a baby shower!" shouted Damien and Riccardo.

"Eric? What do you think? *Eric?*" Angelo asked, tucking at my sleeve as he caught sight of the Elder's warning, and brushed the fear off with a simple smile and a relatively simple sigh.

"What? Oh, yeah, of course..." I came out of my trance to notice Angelo standing close by me. The expression on his face read, *ignore them, and come out of it. We have more important things to do,* about which he was right.

Sophia pulled me closer to her side, shielding me from Santiago and Valentino's eyes. She hugged my arm and while the others discussed the plans of the shower, Sophia laid her head upon my shoulder and whispered quietly to the air.

"It's gonna be wonderful. If I have a son, I'll name him Seth, after the character in my novel. What do you think, Eric?" Her deep brown eyes glanced at me, sparkling with a deadly light that danced from her pupils, at first moving in random, and then gathering into a single glow in the center, like bursting lights filled with wonders.

I parted my lips to speak, but once again the smirk of Santiago and Valentino stopped me from answering her, and froze me in place as I watched them approach us. Santiago walked alongside Valentino, side-by-side like romantic lovers. Like *Louis and Lestat.* Santiago swung the cane slightly to the side, while Valentino used his as the walking stick for which it was meant.

I wasn't afraid of them, and certainly not now that Sophia was beside me observing their every action. The two handsome vampires were a part of the reason this place had done well, though it wasn't the only reason. We had our share of entertaining the crowd. After all, we were the children of the night. People liked the strange and unusual.

Valentino removed his hat, a gentleman in every way, which was the only thing I could ever give him credit for. His long, honey-brown mane was neatly groomed, pulled back in a ponytail. He pressed hard on his lip, tucking it back so that the canines protruded out from within his mouth. His face was painted white with his lips lightly stained red making him a very handsome vampire. The apparel was quite the opposite of the crucified, lace-wearing children of the gothic scene.

Santiago and Valentino had been in this kind of life longer than the rest of us, and wanted no one to forget it.

Santiago removed his hat. His long, black mane was neatly groomed, dangling loosely down his broad shoulders rather than pulled back. Both vampires were quite dashing in their erstwhile vampire style. They were dominating creatures that wanted my position, because they felt they were the elders and entitled to rule over us.

"We- Valentino and I- wanted to do something very special for you, Sophia," Santiago said curving his lip. He tucked the cane under his arm as he spoke.

"Yes," Valentino said inspired by Santiago's words.

They talked one after the other, starting first with Santiago. After his every word Valentino would follow with a few of his own, or finish the sentence for Santiago.

At times, I wondered whether Valentino thought for himself, since he seemed to follow Santiago in every sense of the word. Although he seemed to me like the more dominant vampire, compared to Santiago. Yet in spite of my fears, he followed Santiago without question.

"We'd like to volunteer our time in any way we can, Lady Sophia. This way it won't take time away from Eric's many other tasks."

Tasks? What did they care whether or not I got my job done?

"I agree." Valentino smirked as he bowed his head to Sophia.

The tiny smile on Sophia's face seemed to wither, and she could barely meet their gazes to answer. She was always the shy one, but when it came to Santiago and Valentino, their aggression made her tremble.

Filled with anger, I held back as Sophia's hold on my arm tightened. Had they frozen her into a corner at last? How would she answer to their obvious flirtation; it didn't appear she knew how to reply to such a bogus request. Would she say yes, because she saw no other escape from this? Or was she waiting for me to save her from this confrontation?

"What do you gentlemen suggest?" she finally whispered; it was a wonder they heard her.

"We can take care of you," Santiago suggested, inching closer.

"Very *good* care of you," Valentino continued. "After all, you'll need all the help you can get in your delicate condition."

Sophia's lips tightened, and the smirk on both Santiago's and Valentino's faces grew, until Damien came into the picture. Damien, who was a true friend to Sophia and who always spoke her mind, on just about everything. Dressed in a long black-laced dress and black leather boots, she bounced right into the conversation, ignoring Santiago and Valentino, who couldn't help but shift their bodies to distance themselves from her, as if she had a rare disease.

She wore all sorts of crucifixes crowding her narrow neckline; black eyeliner made up her brown eyes, and her lips were caked in a bright bold red. Pale like the others, a ghost in black satin and lace, with long black gloves and rings on every finger, a regular child of the night. She smiled, flashing the double canines from the parted, painted lips of her mouth.

"I'm afraid that position has already been filled, gentlemen," I said, as Damien took hold of Sophia's hand and pulled her away from us.

"Sorry, guys. Excuse us," Damien uttered, giggling.

Damien made faces at the Elders as she dragged Sophia with her. No one was more qualified for the job than her, and she was going to make sure everyone knew that.

The ladies, along with Riccardo, disappeared through the office doors; only Angelo, Damon, and I were left to eye the growling Elders. All the guys were standing tall, like roosters in a hen house.

Again, the same grimace dropped from Santiago's face, flooded with envy and jealousy. He charged closer, seeming to disappear in the pale office light, staring me down. Heat from his breath touched my cold cheek, as I stood inches from him. I backed off without expressing a speck of fear. Such an indication would surely have given him a tiny victory. People like him couldn't stand anyone like me, a child of lace, to tell them what to do.

"I would watch my step if I were you, Eric," Santiago threatened, curving his lip and smirking slightly.

"Is that a *threat?*" I couldn't get over the fact that my reaction to this impasse was to be this other man's, if you could call him a man.

His eyes flared from their sockets like hot marbles, and his nostrils were wide and expending in the same exact style.

He pushed the stringy bits of hair from his face, lifting his head up and tossing the strands back. Holding his gaze, he stepped back a slight bit, sighing; then, he grinned.

"You must be jealous that Sophia will lose interest in you. That she will come to realize what a loser you truly are. Or are you simply noticing that she finds me more attractive? Which one is it, Eric?"

"*Attractive?* Let's get something straight here, Santiago. Sophia happens to be married to our boss, Nathan. If she finds anyone attractive, it's him, not you, nor I for that matter."

He smirked. "It doesn't matter. Sophia can't deny her true feelings for me. Just like every other woman, single or married, they all want me. She's no different; she's just more gorgeous."

"He's jealous." Valentino sneered.

Boiling angry, I shoved against him, baring my fangs in a snarl. How dare he speak of Sophia like that?

"You have a lot of nerve after all she's done for us! Why can't you respect her? *You bastard!*"

"Back off, Eric!" Santiago growled, spreading his lips back and flashing his own fangs at me.

"*Jealous,*" Valentino mocked from beside Santiago.

"I suppose he is." Santiago gleamed; the snarl on his face vanished, and he regained his composure once more. Nonetheless, it was the twisted smile of a demented, or at least tormented, demon.

"We've never fought with one another, maybe the norms, but

never one another." Damon said trying to extinguish the flare between us. He stepped beside us. "Let it go," he firmly said.

"Yeah, no one is better, we're all equal here. We stand for the same things. Why can't you two just accept that?" Angelo asked, stepping alongside me.

His long, bluish-white hair came down over his shoulders, glittering from his head. His eyes were white, sparkling, while his face was painted in a whitely glimmered shimmering shine. He was the vast, throbbing and overpowering whiteness of us all. He sparkled like a disco ball, so it didn't come to anyone's surprise why we called him "Disco Angelo," or why others would call him Disco Vampire.

"We're not the same! Not with you! Not with any of you! I should be leading this coven. I shouldn't be told what to do by a bunch of children in lace!"

"Children?" mumbled Damon, glancing back at Angelo.

"Did he just call us *children?*"

Angelo shrugged his shoulders.

I stepped back, with a smile across my face.

"So, this is what it's all about?" I paused, still looking at Santiago. "Listen, Santiago, Sophia chose me. That was her decision."

"An easy mistake. I don't blame her," he rudely uttered, allowing the attractive Spanish accent to slip from his dry mouth.

"Do I have to remind you what happened when Sophia granted your wish? You fell on your ass miserably. Remember that?"

Long ago, Sophia had given all the tasks to Santiago, that errant member who claimed he wanted for some responsibility and leadership. He was given my position for a month.

When he discovered he had to work, he was distraught. What did he think a leader did? He discovered he had to write the checks for the bills of the Cathedral, plus other miscellaneous bills, then deal with the vamps' allowances, plus the liquor orders had to be filled, as well as help Sophia schedule all the appointments and duties.

After a month of this, he quit, leaving me to deal with the mess;

luckily for me, I had already taken care of most of the things. It wasn't a big deal.

Santiago glared straight at me with fire erupting from his eyes and face. Angelo and Damon came to stand beside me, and made their vampire grins visible to Santiago. Their tall gangly forms shadowed behind me protectively, as a shield from the menacing Elders. A friendly vampire warning, that's all it was. When one bares his fangs, it can mean a whole lot of things. In this case it meant, *back off!*

It makes you question why the Elders ever put up with all of it. Oh, sure they could have left, rather than put up with a younger vampire bossing them around, but that was never an option for Santiago or Valentino. I mean, where would they go? Sophia gave them everything, a generous allowance to do as they pleased, a place to sleep, independence the outside world couldn't offer them. They ate here; they partied here and played. This was home, a real home.

Believe me, they weren't stupid. All they had to do was be themselves, with no one to tell them they couldn't.

Santiago's eerie chuckle startled me. His grimace suddenly revealed his fangs to me, and a very faded hiss dropped from his parted mouth. A sure sign he was willing to go with the flow for as long as it took.

The two vampires strolled out the office doors, with Santiago holding onto Valentino's arm tightly; tall and standing proudly, the two Elders left the room with their hideous chuckling fading behind them.

Again, the same thought came into my mind as before: if only Ramiel were here. Just then Angelo said those very same words.

"Man, if Ramiel were here, he'd put those two in their *place...*"

"No doubt about it, *Angelo.*"

————

I EDGED near the door and took a peek inside. I caught sight of Mr. Abuda at the very end of the office, seated in the leather chair that had once belonged to his mother, Sophia. I stepped back, afraid to enter, and for a second, I couldn't make myself go inside. I wanted to walk away, but he spotted me immediately and there was no luck of escaping now.

Slowly, I stepped in, nervously trembling, and desperately trying to hide the fact that I was. I walked over to his desk and stood quietly in front of him.

Mr. Abuda silently was looking over some business documents. He didn't rise nor grin, or even say hi. Mr. Abuda never grinned. His dark hair fell slightly over his pale face. He was a man who was mostly withdrawn, and barely smiled. His face lay vacant; human expressions were saved only for his mother.

As a matter of fact, some of the others have come to call him "the Prince" because he reminded them of his mother's fictional character in her novels. The one who didn't smile. The coldhearted fiend with expressions made of stone. The occasional smirk only to send fear into the hearts of others. If he ever found out what he was called, I feared what his reaction would be.

Yet we treated him like a little brother. The Vampire Elders had given him all their guidance and wisdom. No matter how remote they had appeared to us, they had taken the time to shape the handsome form that had now come to frighten us all. It had never been their fault or his. Why he had turned out so cruel? I could never answer that.

We all loved him from the very moment he was born, and for that reason it strangely puzzled me that I feared him. Why was I nervous when in his presence? He had changed in some way or another, my senses kept assuring me. There was something different about him that couldn't be placed.

———

I CLOSED MY EYES; the sounds around me were familiar, as well as the smells surrounding me. Only when I opened my eyes again did I find myself in that hospital, sitting with the others, waiting.

I rose from the seat with great excitement, my heart beating wildly against my chest. The others rose with me, watchful and alert, hoping to see the nurse appear and announce the new Prince of the Cathedral. But no nurse arrived, and the excitement seemed to die from their faces as nurse after ghostly nurse passed us by without a word of Sophia's condition.

Santiago and Valentino were by themselves again, a distance from the group, once more gazing out the windows of the second-floor building. They were just as excited, but showed us very little of their eerie happiness. Though already well beyond their made-up faces, I could almost detect their plans with the baby. Perhaps a growing need to teach him in their ways, to have him hate us and to have him obey them. To cautiously foster the little Prince that would one day take his father's place in the Cathedral; I was hoping that this would prove well for them. To earn his approval now would surely be wise.

The nurse finally came; she appeared in the long hallway, flagging us down as we rose to rush to her side. As she approached, her eyes widened, and she stared up and down at us. It took a couple of seconds for her to gather the words.

For a moment she stared blankly at us, examining our costumes. I wasn't surprised, but was too used to the idea of people staring to let it bother me. The others, though younger, felt the same way, but at times had a way of making people feel stupid.

"Take a picture, it'll last longer," Damien remarked.

The others just laughed out loud, but it seemed the naïve nurse had barely heard anything before she snapped from out of her trance.

She gazed at me, the only one not laughing, the only one smiling warmly up at her with any modicum of human understanding. The only one friendly enough to hush the others, with a simple and benevolent snap of my fingers. Could this be the leader? Her confused face seemed to question.

Santiago and Valentino had already hurried to the huddling cowl of black lace and crucifix-wearing children of the night and were a step behind, staring and looking menacing at the woman.

"Eric?" She asked trembling, "Are you *Eric?*" Her voice was shaky, with a difficult smile forming upon it. She didn't know what to make of us; most didn't. I blamed ignorance; others would blame the attire.

"Yes, that is I," I answered in my most sinister tone of voice.

"Are they all with you, too? You are with the Abuda family?"

"Yes..." I answered, my voice hissing and revealing the canines from the folds of my lips. "Can we see our *Lady?*"

Again, she seemed to awaken as if from a trance, her eyes gazed back up at mine. Once again there was laughter from the others, who flashed their fangs at her in their grins.

"Yes, please follow me," her voice croaked with great difficulty and tribulation rising barely above their laughter.

I turned and eyed the others, snapping my fingers for their volunteered silence. They obeyed as we walked down the hospital hallway, aiming ourselves straight towards Sophia's unit.

The nurse led us to a single room at the end of the hallway, where it was silent and quite abandoned, a perfect spot for privacy.

As we entered, I saw Nathan seated next to Sophia's bed, Sophia was sitting up, and in her arms, she held her baby.

Damien and the others raced to her side to catch a look at the Young Prince.

I took my turn after all the others had their turn, gazing down at the lovely boy in Sophia's arms. Only when Sophia called me to sit by her did I get to hold him. No one had been given such an honor; of all the other vamps, I was the only one, and yet none of the others were jealous.

I held the baby in my arms carefully with Sophia's help; the others crowded us and kneeled around me, taking turns touching and patting his wicked black nest of hair. He was a lovely boy, so tiny with the thickest, most nebulously ebony nest of hair on his head, even for an infant. So plump, as small and tiny as a peach, pink and soft as a rose petal. His hair was soft like silk, placid like a gentle feather. Whatever temptations were there, I neatly held in total check.

He stirred only for a second in my embrace. Through his tiny mouth a small yawn escaped, and even his tiny tongue poked out from his protruding, moist lips, with insignificant tendrils of twisting drool bubbling from his bottom suctioning tool. He was more than ready to nurse.

Away in sleep he remained, huddled like plum trees swept over from the mighty wind, with those enormous ruddy cheeks making his cute, little bottom lip stick out. He was adorable.

"He's beautiful," I whispered to Sophia, who capably and primly smiled.

Only when I stared up at her did I catch the eyes of the Elders by the end of the bed, clearly waiting their turns. Their rightful turns, they had always argued and fought for so well.

"May we see him, Lady Sophia?" Santiago politely asked, over the whispers and the laughter of all the others, who were examining the baby beside me.

Sophia slowly turned and froze with their shadowy presence, then nodded, as did the other vamps.

"Eric?" Sophia turned to me. I nodded, rose with the baby in my arms and walked over to them carefully, and very slowly. Much too slowly for my own personal comfort.

The others gazed up and rose to watch the approval of the Elders at that moment. It was as if without their approval, young Seth, Prince already of this great realm, would not get what was by birth rightfully his. By the law in Vampire Reality, the Elders had their say-so, and their opinions. Though the others mightn't like them, and even if they liked to think otherwise, the Elder's opinions mattered. And their blessing was as important as the belief that their rich blood would give you their power.

Again, the baby stirred in my arms, but never opened his eyes or awakened from its slumber. Santiago came closer and touched the infant gently on his forehead, drawing a pentagram with his finger. He swiftly tilted the baby's black nest of hair back, and indicated to Valentino the small but noticeable *widow's pike-* a true notion of his vampiric inheritance.

After further examining the baby, Valentino nodded and gave the infant his blessing again by drawing the special and perverse pentagram in the air over the baby's forehead. Finally, Santiago blessed him with a Satanic prayer, and kissed his head softly. Like a priest, Santiago ended his prayer; as the others softly whispered the same words, ending the prayer with a most complete act of rejoice.

––––––

I looked around the office—it was different now, in a way. The old meeting table was gone and in its place was a large desk with a cherry finish. Against the wall, there were bookshelves and a variety of books on the occult, the vastly unsolved mysteries, and that sort of hideous rot. A shiny wooden floor had replaced the carpet, and though there was no carpet now, a few cashmere rugs lay beneath the two leather chairs in front of Mr. Abuda's desk, and underneath it.

Mr. Abuda didn't once look up at me. Instead, he ignored me the whole time, as I stood there like a fool waiting for him to acknowledge me. Once satisfied that he had read the entire papers' contents, he placed the pages aside, then lifted his eyes up to me. The cruel, cold, hard features of a gentleman with paralyzing eyes and an insensitive stare beckoned me from the other side of the desk.

I could see how much he resembled his Father. He had a neatly trimmed haircut, yet a portion of his long black bangs dangled over his widow's peak, and his large black eyes were shaped like almonds, with dark, thick eyebrows arched slightly upward. His lips were full, slightly reddened, and moist, while his cheekbones sank into his face, darkening his features.

Handsomely wicked and dashing, he had modeled in Business

Week, Gentleman's Quarterly, and other such magazines as one of Houston's richest, most successful, and handsomest available bachelors. For weeks, women called to speak with him, in hopes of setting a date with him. But for Mr. Abuda, if it wasn't business, he had no interest in it. He had ordered all his admirers away, scolded the magazine editors for paralyzing his business, and threatened to sue for bad interpretation of character. Editors apologized and published another article, this time an article on his mother and her growing Empire. This pleased Mr. Abuda, and the editors were happy that they were capable of doing so.

"What is it?" Mr. Abuda suddenly snapped.

I stepped back; my heart skipped a beat as I gazed directly at him. The look on his face was dry, expressionless.

The full lids of his eyes dropped slightly as he curved his brows impatiently, and his eyes disappeared beneath them.

"Yes?" he pushed on, parting his moist, full lips beautifully. It made me sick that he was so attractive. I felt his eyes examine me carefully the whole time.

Mr. Abuda frightened me, simply because he was so cold and so heartless and so goddamned good at it.

"Ralph...said you wanted to see me?" I nervously answered with my voice shaking. I couldn't help it.

Mr. Abuda frowned and sat back in his chair, thinking about the reason that he had called me in, then as if recalling he asked that I take a seat. He didn't hesitate, and came to the point immediately.

"Did you hire a new bartender?" Mr. Abuda firmly asked, wrinkling his brow slightly up at me.

The tone of his soft voice rose.

"Why yes. I thought we could use a new bartender, since Angelo needs occasional weekends off, and no one knows how to do his job as well as he does. The other barkeep we hired only works part-time, and our full-time bar back has already given his two-weeks-notice."

Mr. Abuda tapped his fingernail on the desk, and then pushed his work aside, almost overcome with frustration. He took a quick sip from the cup of coffee sitting on his desk, pushing back his long bangs over his adult, unblemished widow's peak, and then glanced straight at me again.

"How am I to perform my duties if I have incompetent employees such..." I heard him say. It was a question he seemed to be asking himself, but said loud enough that I could hear it.

"May I remind you, Eric...?" Mr. Abuda scolded, leaning forward, his lips curved and the smirk that had always framed his face returning to remind me.

As Angelo had once said, he knew me. He was only using the vampire way of speech, one which inexorably transfixes me in its embrace.

"You have no authority to hire anyone without my say so."

It seemed he hadn't heard anything I had said. Or had no desire to begin his own perambulations of pity.

"But I do all the hiring. I always have. And I've never had any problems before."

Mr. Abuda rose from his chair. I shifted on my seat nervously as he hovered over me from the other side of the desk. He was a very tall man, taller than me, taller than any man I had laid eyes on and greater than any, for that matter. His monstrous height frightened me, and only now that I sat before him did I realize how eerie and unreal his form seemed.

"When I started working in this position, I was hired to do one thing, and that was to take charge of things; in order to help keep this place active and productive. I suggest you get used to the idea of change. From now on, you must get authorization from me to hire anyone. Is that understood?"

"Yes, sir." I nodded, wanting to rise and leave, but he hadn't finished with me.

"This person you hired. When is he or she...expected?" Mr. Abuda asked, walking from around his desk with his arms behind his back.

He stepped in front of the windows of the office that overlooked the foyer, and the narrowly wide antechamber of the large Cathedral, examining the interior. He was wearing a navy Armani suit with a red tie, which laid over his spreading breast flatter than a pancake. The cologne from his body smelled of Ralph Lauren's Romance, which was his father's most favorite fragrance.

"He will be training with Angelo this weekend, sir," I managed to utter through quivering lips.

"Training? Time is a luxury we can't afford, and a waste of money." His noble form unmoving and wall-like stood with his back to me. It was one of his famous quotes, which never failed to surface. God, how I hated that quote of his.

The poetic doubt in Mr. Abuda's voice made me shake slightly.

"He just needs to know where everything is. But I assure you; he understands precisely how to perform the job. Training would mostly be assuring he knows where everything is on the bar."

But that wasn't the truth, and I knew that. Said "hired hand" had no experience at all, and my only reason for hiring him was because Angelo had begged me, and no one else had taken the job. I figured I could train him on the weekdays, while the Cathedral was not busy. But now the sounds of Mr. Abuda's impatient voice made me doubt whether I would be able to do that without Mr. Abuda's lecturing me later.

Mr. Abuda exhaled, and then turned to face me from where he stood. His handsome, flawless face resembled the attractive Prince of the Sarlovakk Dynasty in his mother's novel. And I couldn't stop thinking how the uncanny resemblance was unmistakable between the two. Yet there was a slight difference between them that was also noticeable, and that was the way they treated people. Anyone who had read her novel would see that.

Though oddly some time ago, Mr. Abuda had helped his mother promote her novel by making an appearance as her character in a private function for a magazine layout. When asked to do it again, he refused. It seemed he had matured incredibly since then, and hardly granted interviews.

"Very well then, but if your foolish decision to hire another person without my permission fails. I will hold you entirely responsible for whatever difficulties arise because of it. You can be the one to inform my mother of why her cathedral finances reflect poor numbers this quarter."

"It won't, sir, I promise."

Mr. Abuda flashed a cruel smirk, and placing his hands behind his back again, turned away from me. "That is all. You may leave."

"Yes, sir." I rose and hurried towards the door.

"Eric, one last thing..."

I turned slightly, stopping by the entrance to look back at him.

"I advise you to get used to the idea of having me in charge. It would be very beneficial to you and the others if I were pleased with your performance come review time."

I wanted to say something in response but didn't as I stepped out of the small office, leaving Mr. Abuda by the window.

I left feeling slightly troubled; my time and hard work had meant nothing. I was simply part of the entertainment, a worker with a number. The coven that had once existed with Sophia was non-existent now. Mr. Abuda's greed and power-hungry hands had silenced the family, and neither Ramiel nor Sophia had intervened, nor stopped it in any way.

I alone could not stop things. I was no one.

2

MOTHER IS THE WORD FOR GOD

SETH

The lie that is known to be a lie...

I observed Eric from the other side of the office window descending the grand staircase slowly and stopped to look back. Eric's ghostly face was painted white, and covered in a milky color. His eyes shaped like almonds were traced in dark outliner, while his lips were plain and stripped of color. A long brush of black hair draped his back and shoulders as he moved down the marble steps of the great fortress, in which his steps echoed as he descended.

Our eyes did not meet through the glass of the office; one could not see the other from the opposite side. Yet we both knew of the other's presence from the other end, standing glaring back.

Eric descend the stairs like a floating pale banshee, reaching the bottom with a pasty thud and walking across the antechamber into a door to his left that led into the vaults.

I crossed my arms, took a breath, and held back a single laugh.

"Eric, you've become such a nuisance. What the hell am I going to do with you?" I announced to the empty room. A chuckle escaped my devilish laughter. "Maybe kill you."

I spun around, to find a figure standing at the entrance of my office. My heart skipped a beat for a moment, then quickly regained my composure to challenge the form. *Who was this now intruding on my time alone?*

I took a step forward away from the window, alert and feeling my heart racing against my chest. The figure was covered in a silhouette by the shape of the door. I hurried a step forward, stopping dead in my tracks. It was only when I was inches away that a radiant face surged from the darkness before me. A pair of brown eyes sparkled from the shapeless blackness. I shuddered, unwilling at their presence.

A glowing seemed to glimmer from her smooth, creamy skin, as a smile greeted me and spread in delight. Only then did I realize I was staring into the beautiful face of Sophia, the Lady of the Cathedral.

Dressed in a red, long silk dress, her long brown hair draped behind her as she moved into the room. She wore no make-up, only a glossy lipstick that shimmered from her full mouth. She didn't look a day older in comparison to the picture on my desk that had been taken when I was only ten. It was almost as though she had never aged. I never found that disturbing. It had only engrossed me the more and inspired the veil of most delicate and delectable fantasies.

I clumsily walked to her side. I felt weakened by her presence, and beckoned by her beauty. Her perfume awakened my senses, and I gazed dreamily at her. A scent of fruit lured me to her lips, and I had to shake myself awake.

She gazed at me puzzled, her small rounded face glowing in the twilight of her smile. I wanted to reach out and caress her ready cheek but, as always, refrained from doing so. Why all these restraints?

"My...Lady." My lips quivered, losing control.

I hated the idea of the word *mother*. I had never thought much about it. It had never felt right. For those reasons, I couldn't bring myself to use it any longer. There was something growing between us, a bond deeper than anyone could ever comprehend. I didn't understand it at first, but slowly I welcomed the feelings and had come to finally accept them. We were connected in a manner beyond this reality. In my dreams, we were far more. Everything in them was coming true.

Dizzy, I balanced myself as she came closer. Her perfume affected me in far more ways than I had predicted. I was much too fragile a thing. To be near her frightened me. I was weaker than I had first realized, and I couldn't resist her. Was it her scent what lured me, or the scent of something far primal?

"Mother," I reluctantly corrected myself, observing frown lines of disappointment displayed upon her gentle face. She had a sweet, flawless face, almost angelic and childlike in appearance.

I parted my lips, dazed and under her spell. I bent forward to place a single kiss upon her cheek. My heart throbbed and erupted with desire. I pulled away a step back.

"To what do I owe the honor of your visit?" I examined her with curiosity; she was such an innocent beauty.

My eyes could not resist the inviting textures of her lovely skin. She took a breath and I watched as she exhaled.

"Do I need a reason to see you, darling?" she answered with a sweet smile.

Her youthful appearance fooled others, but never me; she acted like a wiser person but appeared the sweet age of a younger *girl* one would see among the high school halls.

"No...of course not..." I bit my lips as the word left my mouth in a whispered to faint to hear, but I dared not say it out loud again.

The sounds of breathing and heavy moans echoed beyond a place I kept secret, a woman with red hair lay beneath me as I came down over her. Her face, I could not clearly see at first, but as I neared it became clear and I came...*Sophia!*

She wanted me, and I knew it. In one swift moment she drew me in. Did she even know it? This woman...*in my dreams?*

I reached forward as the image left my thoughts and held her to me. She wrapped her arms around me and held me in the same manner.

I need you, my mind repeated, *I need you just as much as you need me...*

I felt the firmness of her body as she squeezed me close and exhaled. The same woman was now staring down at me as she neared the side of my bed. In my dreams, I could never see her face, only when she near. This time she mounted me, and I saw her face...

"Is something troubling you?" she asked.

I fought my orgasm, the image of *her* beneath me penetrated my thoughts so cruelly. I desperately tried to resist, but the more I did. The more I felt it drew me in, there was no escaping the desires, or the idea that something else was in control, something divine, or something powerful beyond my comprehension.

"Nothing to concern yourself with...I must just be overworked." My lips trembled.

No, that's not the truth. I love you. I want you.

I moved aside; the discomfort was drawing us apart. She gazed at me as I turned to smile at her, extending my hand as I did to assure her everything was well.

A light sheen of sweat dampened my brow as I rewarded her with a grin. She took my hand and I helped her over to a seat near my desk. She seemed to shake a slight bit.

I walked around the chair where she sat, to stand next to the desk, and observed her like a lost puppy.

Sophia met my gaze briefly. She looked frozen in time regarding her age. In fact, she looked my age.

"I just wanted to come in here and tell you that your father is returning soon. He called earlier in the morning," Sophia managed to say, stumbling upon her words.

"So, the call earlier...that was him?"

I was aware of the call. I had heard his voice at the other end. I meant to speak, but Sophia's voice answered before I could. Instead of putting the phone down, I listened.

I miss you, he said. *I love you....* The very words I wanted to say myself. I knew that I felt the same way.

I wanted to express those same desires, those same feelings. My lips had parted and had begun to speak. But for whatever reason, I said nothing...silence.

"Why didn't you want to talk to him?" asked Sophia softly, gazing over at me.

Had she sensed my dislike for the man?

"He asked about you..."

Had she heard me on the other end? I thought, thinking back on that morning when I had softly put the phone down. Then, I'd dropped back on the bed, unable to resist grabbing a part of myself to entertain the desires I felt. There was no other way to satisfy the demons and the lust eating at me.

"Did he? Is that the reason of your visit, to lecture me regarding my quarrels and behavior with the man?"

"Seth, *please*. Where is all this coming from? You know he loves you. Why all this animosity?" Sophia lowered her head, knowing how untrue those words now sounded to her. They were all unrehearsed.

I didn't understand it myself. What I felt for him, the anger that had started to emerge at a slow ascend. I felt betrayed, and rage from somewhere in my heart, far more with the idea that he possessed something I desired. I felt I had failed, and that he had a part in my failure. It was because of him that I had lost what I wanted so much.

"We've never been close." It was all I could say in my defense. It was all she might be able to understand. His absence perhaps...as a father. He was always away...But of course there was more, more that she couldn't understand more than I could understand fully, but felt.

I saw the sadness in her eyes. I felt bad for being the one to place it there. For her, I would make an exception. So, I swallowed my pride for her sake, and knelt in front of her, taking her hands into mine.

I love you, I whispered...*forgive me. I've been having dreams...of a past- a meaningful past- that I have not yet put together. But it has something to do with us. We are unique in some way; we are one in another plain. We were once in love. I don't know what happened to us. But I can feel it, can you? All this around us, this—this is the fantasy....*

"Forgive me," I said instead.

"Will you *talk* to him when he returns?"

She lifted her face up. I kissed her hand, she looked naively at me. Sophia's brown eyes sparkled brightly full of innocence. An image of the red-haired woman surfaced in my mind again to provoke desire and stir the lust.

"I will talk with him. I promise," I answered. I was paralyzed, fixed lifelessly on her.

I kissed her hand again and gave her a warm smile.

I stood as she rose, and kissed my cheek. I wrapped my arms around her. Her touch felt devilish and made me keenly excited. I restrained.

"Thank you, my darling," Sophia softly said.

She fell away like dead flowers to look at my face. Her eyes seemed to search for something. I loved it when she looked at me that way. I felt as if she was searching for a part of what I felt inside me that connected us. Instead, she saw this protectively feverish gaze upon my childish face assuring her of my promise. Was she trying to see something else beyond my eyes?

Perhaps how much I looked like him in a way with my hair brushed sideways, dark and maintained. However, I honestly never saw it. We looked nothing alike, because he wasn't my father as much as we wanted to believe that lie. We were pawns in this wicked game. This was all an illusion and we had bought into it. It had to be nothing else. She had, he had, and even at one point, I had believed. But now, no more. In a way, it was separating us a little.

. . .

My eyes followed. Sophia moved discretely away, walking over to the door of the office, and immediately turned. I didn't want her to leave. Our eyes met, and I knew right away she had realized I'd never looked away. My smiled rewarded her in return.

She seemed to shake an idea away, then faced me to announce what troubled her fragile mind. "I wanted to ask you to do something *else* for me," she merely said. Her delicate lips twisted slightly and seemed tense and unsure how to proceed.

Was I making her uncomfortable? I hoped that I had not. It had never been my intentions to do such a thing.

The smile on my face spread further.

Is she remembering...perhaps a part of her past?

"I will do *whatever* you ask," I answered arrogantly, a quick reply she most certainly had not expected or asked for. She wanted my attention for whatever she was about to say, not to be pleased by some love foolish idiot.

She hesitated, trying to find the right reaction to my words. She took a few steps forward. She seemed uneasy. I hated that I had put her in such discomfort. She eased, and I wondered if she thought of him now, if he had been the one to bring her to a state of peace? I hated the idea that his name was one thing that separated me from ever knowing her.

Why did I hate him so much? I felt I could kill him and care nothing for doing so. I just wanted him gone; something in me said he was my enemy. Those feelings were growing with time, evolving far more.

"I want you to be nicer to Eric and the others," she finally said, without any restraint. Where had this come from? Had I been revealed as a tyrant by the group? I wouldn't doubt it; I had been known to dislike their attics, their useless existence within our Cathedral.

"*What?* Nicer, in *what* way?" I stammered, moving from her, hoping to hide my frustration at her discouraging request. "They're... incompetent, I'm sorry to say. No, I'm not sorry. They're costing us money," I finally admitted.

"Seth, please listen to me," she demanded; her lips tightened. She pushed back the long, brown locks of her hair as she tried to deny the fact that my grin had made her blush.

I stared back at her limpidly beautiful and serenely deep brown eyes. She lowered her glance.

She stepped up to me trying to avoid my look. She came close enough that I could smell her perfume again. Her gentle gaze carved my attention; she placed a soft hand over my masculine hands.

I caught my reflection in her endlessly black eyes. I was frozen, paralyzed in that moment. I felt numb standing before her, strangely enough her eyes had grown darker. Almost instantly, they regained their brown color once more.

I pulled slowly away from her gentle embrace, and walked around my desk. I scanned the top, frustrated by her request. I found what I was looking for to prove my point and placed the paper across my desk for Sophia to see. She came to stand in front of the cherry-finished office furniture.

She took a hold of herself, trembling. She was cold. She was a delicate flower and I was a brute at keeping my office chilly. She'd forgotten to wear her shawl.

I pushed the paper forward for her to see.

"Their presence seems unnecessary. They cost us more money to have around. Half of the time they don't know what they're doing. These are the expenses of last month. Why do you allow them to continue here? What is their purpose? This is precisely why I took this position, to correct such mistakes..."

SOPHIA LIFTED the paper from the desk, but unable to stop from shuddering she soon lost interest in the sheet in her hand. She squeezed her body, losing the document from between her cold fingers. She unknowingly gazed up at me briefly before the paper streamed to the edge of the desk. I caught it from falling to the floor.

"Let me..." My lips twisted slightly to one side. I took the document, placing it properly on my desk. I came around, taking my blazer off, and placed it over her.

Sophia smiled up at me, she seemed uneasy and unlike herself. I felt she didn't want to continue the argument, simply because she didn't feel comfortable any longer.

She looked confused. Was she sensing something, remembering something? *Remember*, my mind kept repeating, wanting to tell her. If she could recall, she would know I was someone not to fear, someone that loved her.

"*Mother*," I whispered, paralyzed for a moment.

I felt the warmth of her body, the throbbing of her heart echoing unstoppably as I neared. I was closer in spirit to her then she could possibly know.

Sophia slightly turned away. I leaned closer.

"You don't have to worry. I can take care of everything. They don't have to know it was your decision to let them go," I said.

I felt her breath kiss my lips, the moment a penetrable death was infinitely preferable to this. Her heart rapidly moved inside my head. This, as quickly as the visions of her drawing ever so closely, was gone with the lashing of her quick words.

"You will do nothing of the sort! May I remind you; you were brought here to assist me and not make such hasty decisions. You will let them be!" She wrestled herself from the seat with her back to me.

I wept at her cruel painful words, there had not been an awakening, only a wicked illusion of what I wanted. I had longed for it far too soon.

She faced me. "They're my friends. I love them. I will never do that. How can you even *consider* such a thing after all they've done for you? They took care of you as a child. You *owe* them your respect." She lowered her voice, unable to challenge my eyes.

She took the coat still clinging to her body and held it away. Her eyes indicated she recognize the familiar fragrance upon the fabric. It reminded her of him, *Nathan*, it reminded her of how much she missed him. It was his cologne after all.

SHE APPROACHED, pushing the coat into my hands and headed towards the office doorway. I set the blazer on the chair, never once looking away. I should have apologized, but I couldn't find the right words. I was a fool to say that to her. Of course, she needed time to consider such a convincing argument. She had to first see their stupidity for herself. I didn't want her to think I was an insensitive brute like Nathan. If so, I would never get what I really wanted...

"Please, Seth," she begged stopping midway, her waist-long, brown hair cascading from her shoulders. She was like the dessert I longed to devour at first glance. My, that image was rewarding. How smooth and rich it was, and beckoning for another taste.

I caught tears pooling in her brown eyes as she slightly turned to look back. The pain on her gentle face was obvious. For a second, I examined her feeling I could weave her agony into a more delightful expression, one filled with desires and lust. We were bound, but not by blood, by a past.

"Son?"

I fell out of the trance nearly collapsing into despair. Was she mocking my longings with such cruel words, poking at the reality of this world I now lay trapped in?

I took a step forward. Anger fashioned my expression, and I bit hard at my lip pushing back at the agony at the sound of the words spewing from her precious lips.

"Just be nice to them. Do it for me," she pleaded once again.

My expression softened. I wasn't angry with her, but angry at this separation, this existence.

That's all I had to hear, though. *Do it for me.* Her words mocked, provoked, and invited.

A smile spread over my full lips, feeling the strain of my member pushing against the fabric of my slacks. I grabbed the coat from the chair, to conceal my erection from her.

"Of course, I will, whatever you ask. I love you...*Mother*."

The words left my lips in a release, blood rushed into my veins and I exhaled in ecstasy.

"I love you too, darling," she replied.

I climaxed as she exited the office to leave me alone. I collapsed upon on the leather chair behind my desk dropping the coat on my lap. I lay there consumed with the reality, the pain, and the anxiety of how to best handle my growing desire.

3

DOWNTOWN

Something evil is upon us...something wicked has been unearthed...

The rain poured down the dark, quiet streets of downtown Houston. In one of the lonelier parts of town, a poor homeless man wandered into one of the dark alleys. Hungry, he searched the wasted trash cans for scraps of food, and then took shelter against a corner in the back of an alley. Though the rain had not stopped, he embraced it, lifting his face up into the sky. He hoped he would die soon, and trembled at the thought giddily.

It had been raining for a week, and the hunger could not be silenced. He hugged himself, watching as the rain fell while nibbling on a piece of half-eaten sandwich he had found at the bottom of one of the trashcans.

Above the thunder erupted, and the lightning flashed across the sky.

He foolishly fell against the wall, frightened for a minute—only then did he smirk. The night was quiet, but the sounds of the traffic a distance away competed with the sounds from above. Only the rain and the thunder in the sky were clear to him; nothing else in this place made sense.

He carefully gazed about, examining his new home. The smell of trash surrounded him. It was a smell he had always found comforting, as decisive and real as the shadows and the damp corners where insects crawled alongside his fingers and the dirt became his bed. This was home, home sweet home. The rain falling from the sky was his shower, and the trash bins filled with half-eaten desserts were plentiful all along the city corners. You would think so, too, if you were him.

In the distance he heard steps, and was alarmed. He looked out from where he hid from behind one of the trash bins, but saw nothing. A cat meowed somewhere and he grinned, leaning back against the wall, feeling slightly foolish for ever fearing the darkness. The night was his friend; why should he fear it? Evening time was there to hide him, to protect him from those who did not welcome his kind. He could sleep peacefully in its shadows, and shield himself from those out to harm him.

He was tired, wet, and hungry, but all he could hope for was finding something to eat tomorrow. He tried to close his eyes, but the sounds of raindrops wouldn't let him sleep. He opened his eyes once again, gazed in front of him, and then he noticed it. Had it been there before? He backed up against the wall as close as he could, too afraid to run. What *was* it?

A strange black cloud of smoke drifted closely to him. Was it a rain cloud that had drifted closer to the ground? But clouds didn't do that. Did they? It was then that he noticed something strange coming from out of the mystical, smoky air, and it frightened him some more.

Tiny arms, like tentacles that appeared like stringing veins, surrounded it.

What the hell was it? He tried to move around it, but was too afraid. It drifted closely from above him. Again, he tried to crawl away, but he couldn't scream.

The thing kept coming closer; he was too frightened, too freaked to escape. What could this awful and curious thing be?

Bravely, he managed to scatter away from the thing, but it moved over him!

A crisp sound hummed from out of it, almost like rushing water! At once, he crawled to his feet and began to race away, but tripped, feeling his leg had been caught on something. He tried to cut himself loose, but when he did, he realized the thing was on top of him hovering, and one of its tentacles had his leg.

Blood!

He screamed and struggled as it dragged him back; its slimy body engulfed his head, quickly swallowing him whole.

4

STRANGER IN THE DARK

Indulgence—is living.

Lucas Williams rushed home through the rain. He was upset his car had not started, yet happy that he had finally gotten a job he would surely enjoy. In two days, he would start and perhaps make enough to get the piece-of-shit car fixed. But for now, he had to keep taking the Metro and making the long walk home. The rain hadn't helped, but at least the day wasn't entirely a bad one.

He hated walking at night, hated the homeless people on the street bugging him for change. And also, he hated the whistles from the hookers and the transvestites posing as real women at the corner of Montrose as he passed by.

Who were they fooling with their made-up faces and those bulges, so like bugles, in their crotches? He hated people that stereotyped others, yet he found he was doing that now.

Two men holding hands came from out of the tattoo place; as

they passed by, he tried to ignore them, quickly heading in the opposite direction as they stopped to examine the condom shop nearby.
Why *had* he moved here in the first place? Because it was always easy
to identify with other people, others that were different like him. He
loved the neighborhood. This place had always been his home, a
home for the rebellious and the free-minded thinkers. Libertines
were not something altogether tolerable.

He turned on Westheimer and continued down, passing the Taco
Cabana restaurant; the bars were still open, even though it wasn't the
weekend yet. He could stop and get a drink, but then he knew he
would just waste the rest of his money, and he needed to save it, at
least until he got paid from his new job. He had filled out so many
applications in the local bars, yet he had no experience as a
bartender. So, he was surprised when the Cathedral de Los
Vampiros, a local club on Westheimer, had called back requesting an
interview, promising to train him. Was it his lucky day, or what?

He had been up late the night before. The beginning of the day
had been filling out applications, and the rest slacking off just a tiny
bit, knowing that somehow, he would have a job the next day. Luckily
for him, it had been so. If not, he would have been fucked.

The phone rang about six pm; it was not surprising he was still in
bed. He grabbed the phone at the fifth ring, falling while reaching for
it. His bedroom was dark; he had covered the windows so well it was
hard to see inside the room even in the daytime.

With the phone in his hand and still asleep, he answered with his
best speaking voice. That frog wouldn't get out of his throat, though.
It leapt around, making phlegm, and felt like another kind of bulge,
indeed.

A soft voice came from the other end of the phone. A male's
voice, polite but clear, penetrated the end of the phone line.

"Hello. Can I speak to Mr. Lucas Williams?"

He almost fell over the side of the bed, fighting his way out of the
sheets, and stood in the room with the phone pressed against his ear,
listening closely.

He hadn't realized how the sound of his name, the manner in which he was referred to by another human being as a "mister," made him feel important. "Speaking," he said, roughly clearing his throat.

"This is Eric, of the Cathedral De Los Vampiros. You filed an application with us the other day. I was just getting back with you. I wanted to say, you have some interesting skills, but not exactly bartender skills."

This statement was enough to bring about its desired effect. He had been a fool to even consider that the job would be his with no experience. It would have been nice to work there; he'd heard so much about the place. It seemed just as hard to get a job there as it was to get in. The place was always busy; he could imagine the tips he would make.

There were probably millions of other bartenders trying to get a job in the Cathedral. What made him think he had any sort of chance in getting the job, especially there?

Disappointed, he felt like ending the conversation, saying, "I understand," and whatnot. There was no way of denying his lack of skills, but he sensed the assurance in Eric's tone. That brightened him considerably.

"But I *think* we can work something out. If you're...*interested?*"

"Yes, of course!" he blurted, only to lower his voice. He didn't want to sound too desperate, either. Unfortunately, he sounded like the proverbial Hades victim, too ready to die to get the job, unready to actually perform it, but he sorted of knew better about that.

"Great," Eric said from the other end of the phone line.

There was little to no emotion in this voice Lucas heard. Were all goths this dislocated with the world? The fact that they were self-proclaimed blood suckers had to be one reason.

Though it sounded sincere enough to him, the awkwardness was there and obviously, it was the awkwardness another feels when talking to a stranger for the first time. At least, he told himself this little, sweet lie.

"I would like you to come in for an interview. What's the best time for you?"

Lucas stumbled, and almost lost his balance, clearing his throat again, and then regained his posture. He pulled himself from out of the sheets. The last end of the thing was strangling him somewhat. At the last second, he pulled away, just in time.

"Anytime! May I come in today?"

The fellow at the other end became silent; he heard one or two muffled voices in the background, then Eric answered.

"How about this weekend? I have an opening, is that fine with you?" again, his voice sounded dry of emotion and slightly insensitive.

"That's great! What time?"

"Let's say around two-thirty am. We don't usually get up until six pm. We are vampires, you know." Eric slightly chuckled, as the words left his lips. It was the first indication of any emotion in his voice. Lucas thought,

Right...

Lucas could imagine what Eric might have appeared like, seated in a dark, dank room with no lighting watching horror movies, drinking from a goblet with some sort of red liquid made to appear like blood, a cloak draping his frame, his face painted white, and porcelain canines revealed beneath the fold of his mouth as his lips parted in a smile.

He could imagine him, with long black hair, and red burning lips, dressed in gothic clothing. Perhaps wearing silver crucifixes, and other jewelry around his neck and upon each finger.

"I hope that's okay with you?"

Only when he heard Eric's voice at the other end did Lucas realize the silence between them. "Oh yes, of course."

It was all ok with him. He was only up now because he had gotten the call from Eric. He loved the idea of getting up late. He could take the idea of sleeping in. It was like a dream job. These people would "help" him.

"I hate the daylight myself, it's only the night life for me, you get me, man?"

"Good, then. I'll expect you between two and two-thirty am. Weekend's our busiest time, but Angelo will teach you the ropes. He's the best. See you then. Bye for now."

He hung up the phone, Lucas muttered quizzically to himself, and stumbled back into his bed with a viciously huge smile spreading across his face. Now, he didn't have to find another apartment, and wouldn't have to leave the neighborhood he had loved so much. He fell asleep like a big baby.

———

THAT HAD BEEN the call that had set things into motion again for him. Buttoning his collar, on time to the very minute, he hurried down the eventful streets, but the local bars were not as busy as he had thought. They were deserted on the weekends, because of the Cathedral De Los Vampiros, and it was no different today.

It wasn't raining as bad as it had been earlier in the day. He walked down the dark streets; a few homeless people were sitting on the sidewalk, lifting their filthy paws up for change, yet he pretended not to see them. He passed them up like they weren't there. He didn't want to look at them.

Why didn't they just get a job? *Bastards,* he thought, at least he was making something of himself, and all they wanted to do was leech off of him.

He continued to walk. Home seemed miles away, but at least the rain had come to a lonely and futile ending.

It was only after a few blocks that Lucas noticed a single figure lingering behind him, one of the homeless, he thought. Ignoring the figure, he continued down the sidewalk, striding faster. He wanted to get to his bed, crawl under the sheets, and close his eyes. For *good.*

But again, he turned, and there was the figure, still close but not visible, behind. *What does he want?* Lucas thought to himself. He faced facts and challenged the form in the dark and quiet streets. The sounds of the city and Montrose were quite a distance away, now. Even if he wanted to cry out, no one would have heard him through the club music or the racket surrounding the area.

"I have no change!" he yelled, but the figure didn't answer, nor did it stop.

Nervously, Lucas walked faster, trying to get away from him, it, or whatever, but the figure continued to follow. He walked faster- no, not *frightened,* but frustrated and tired. He didn't want to deal with these people; at least, not today.

"Later, man!" he screamed aloud.

He almost tripped in his running haste, turned another dark and tangential corner, found the street darker than expected, but he continued. His heart was thumping inside his chest. He gasped, and then stopped. What the hell was he *doing?* He should set this guy straight. If he didn't now, they would never leave him alone; walking home would be a bigger chore. He couldn't let these "people" push him around. *Shit,* who said they were even, well, *people?*

The figure turned the corner, too; it was quiet, the place was deserted. All the houses in the neighborhood seemed deserted and vacant. The sounds of Montrose drifted the semblance of light years away from where he was standing now.

"Fuck off; I said, I have no change!"

The figure didn't say a word, but continued to approach. Lucas couldn't make his face out, but could tell it was a huge, gangly man, with large arms and a broad chest. Or was it, frightfully peculiar, a broad *breast?* The man stopped a distance from him; the shadows hid his features.

Lucas stepped back—there was something eerie about the form, something not right, and something not human.

He tried to run, but he couldn't move. Something had him and he turned his head back just to see it. The figure was approaching inch-by-inch and yard-by-yard. It was time to panic at last, to make a last-minute escape.

He manfully panicked, but the weird tentacle was wrapping around him holding him back. And then, it was too late.

Blood!!

5

UNCONTAINED DESIRES

SETH

Love is overrated...

I entered the bedroom. In the distance, the shower was running. The place was quiet except for the sounds of water and a gentle, soft voice humming. I leaned toward the bathroom door and looked inside. The door was open slightly, but I didn't enter. I caught a sight of her blurry, naked figure through the glass door of the shower. I'd forgotten why I had come, but now her naked form stirred and awakened desires I had hoped to bury at least for now. It just didn't matter any longer.

The strain beneath my pants returned, alive and growing. I exhaled with the exquisite pang of sheer arousal. A smiled curved a corner of my full lips as I drew over to the shower to watch a little more. Then, with an enormous attack of guilt, I moved from the door as Sophia's hand appeared through the open glass, reaching for a plush, purple towel draped over its rack. I caught only a glimpse of one youthful breast when she had reached for the towel.

I moved across the large bedroom, walking by the curtains to lurk in the shadows of the large bedroom. A single light was burning dimly, so it was impossible to make out any shadows among the shapes of the curtains.

My long fingers felt at the growing lump beneath the fabric as my eyes caught her exiting the bathroom. She was wearing a dark, mahogany red robe.

She didn't see me, as I stood across the room behind the dark shapeless curtains of the bedroom. The passion grew with each second and it was getting harder and harder to resist what I longed to do. Why was I here? What did I expect to have happen? I knew exactly what I desired and wanted.

Sophia walked to the mirror and picked up the brush on her dresser, then slowly began to brush her long dark hair. She stopped, putting the brush down, and opened her dresser taking out a pair lacy, colorful, sexy garments.

She walked to the bed and set the exotic bits of lace on the mattress. Then, she pulled open at the robe. I wet my lips, my eager eyes wide, a smile spread like a greedy man counting gold coins.

She took the robe off, and set it aside, taking one skimpy bra from the bedside and worked her arms through the loops.

I watched with growing eagerness, taking note of every inch of her body. The desire below grew, and I didn't know how I could contain it further. Moments earlier, I had come seeking her guidance, her attention, but now that very idea was a faded thought long forgotten.

Instead, I took note of her firm figure. If she knew of prying eyes, she would have hurried to dress herself.

She had soft features, and well-rounded breasts. This was the vehicle that had carried life into my being, had cursed my very existence into this plain. And had very well twisted the meaning of true love. I was not a monster in lust; I was lost in this very moment, but not for perverse reasons, because I had been unleashed into a world our love could not connect and not be taboo in some sense. They knew nothing, I cried from within.

I wanted to feel her close. To feel her firm body, her breasts against my skin and feel their perfection.

She tossed the bra aside and moved onto the next garment. I cared not, as long as she stayed naked and breathing. Nothing in Heaven or on Earth could be a more wonderful sight. She was too young, too vibrant and alive to waste on anyone else.

She grabbed at the panties from the bed and slipped her feet in slowly, lifting each leg slightly. I caught every feature of her form, from every angle.

I groaned with raw desire, such agony. I grabbed at myself, exhaled, and licked at the opening of my gapping mouth.

She stopped. I froze, unable to contain the pleasure of my own hand, or the friction of my moving palm. She glanced across the room, just as I exhaled in agony. I would have collapsed but nothing made sense, not pleasuring one's self, but pleasuring the only one thee loved, no doubt. I found her eyes looking in my direction the, shapeless shadow behind the curtain holding a grip of himself. Her eyes blinked back. Was she unsure of what she had seen?

There was no hiding from the cruel dark desires in the both of us. I stepped out into the open found her eyes gazing back at me. She staggered back, grabbing at the robe from the bed to cover herself. She froze, now unable to move away any further as I came even closer and stood in front of her. The wet of my comings quite obvious on the fabric of my slacks. The sweat of my brow clearly visible, I was exhausted, but no doubt could continue if the invitation was there. My eyes welcomed the summons.

I took the blazer off, pulling at the tie and tossed them on the bed, and moved upon her immediately. Her body stiffened as my arms gripped a hold of her. She trembled; her lips quivered in my hold. Before she could scream, I kissed her, ripping the robe from her grasp and dropping it to the floor.

She desperately struggled in my arms at first as I pressed her naked body against mine, kissing away an aching passion that had been growing. She couldn't fight my misplaced desires, and I couldn't resist her any longer.

I ran my hands over her naked body, pressing her soft breasts, feeling their tenderness against my chest. Strangely, she stopped struggling. I gazed down at her, and in her eyes, I saw it, an intoxicating energy I had felt in myself. She gazed at me, panting- weakened and lost. there was confusion upon her face, but an eagerness to welcome this pleasure that was now pouring from her gaping mouth.

She exhaled, a faint whisper poured from her parted mouth. "We can't...we can't do this terrible thing. It's not right." Her voice was like tendrils of cancerous smoke.

I smiled and gently lay her down upon the bed, bending over her and unfastening my trousers.

She lay still, and seemed far gone, intoxicated even. I lowered myself over her, came down, and pushed gently inside her, pushing hard into her wet and tight cunt. She mumbled again, as I pushed deeper into her, feeling the nectar of her soak my skin.

"We can't...we can't."

But I knew she wanted this I could see it in her eyes! She *wanted* it just as much as I.

"It *is* right...I love you." I whispered, tunneling into her, it was a pleasure I had longed to feel! A pleasure I had felt I had to fight or lose to another. "I need you," I gasped in ecstasy. "I've longed for you. We belong together. Don't you feel it, my love?" I nearly collapsed, the fluttering of my heart exploding in devilish desire. As I felt the ecstasy of my flower opening to my very male essence.

She reached up pulling lose at the garment that dressed me. Tearing away at the opening of the silk shirt from my body her hands reached out and touched me. I yanked it off and fell forward against her breasts and devoured her mouth. She whimpered at my caress and at my kisses, all the pleasure and agony of denying these feelings exploding repeatedly from us. She cried in girlish whimpers as she pressed me to her and stroked the backside of my buttocks.

Moans escaped her gaping mouth in musical releases. Struggles forgotten, she gave in enough to strongly press me to her. I was smiling with the half-grin of a guilty man of deep arousal and passion. Her resistance withered, her pleas and struggles were overlooked. Only now desire, our cries and the sheer pleasure of our lovemaking pounded the walls of the bedroom and rocked the very bed.

I pleasured every part of her body, brought her to the moment of ecstasy repeatedly. Every guilt-ridden moment of desire that I had once longed for now I could take delight in. She was mine at last; she was mine!

Sweat draped the brow of my forehead, the scent of sex was ripe in the room like a cloud, a fragrance of lust. I was soaked in ecstasy, in woman nectar. I smelled her on me, and it kept me a prisoner to her embrace. She took me in, her arms wrapped around me as her lips found my wet mouth. Her tongue pushed and parted my lips hungrily. She was just as hungry as I, if not far more.

She climaxed yet again. I collapsed falling against her, holding her tightly in my arms.

She cried out like a lost goddess in delight, holding my firm buttocks in her hands, pushing me into the very core of her sex. I released in a devilish victory!

"It is *right*," I whispered parting her mouth with my tongue and kissed her. "You're mine, Sophia. You have always been mine. You've only forgotten."

She didn't speak, only exhaled in delight beneath me. I lifted away from her, and sat upon the bed to examine her. On her brow laid a cold sweat, her body was moist and wet, her hairy cherry was glistening, soaked in my come. I touched her pussy, stroked at the opening, driving my finger into her. She groaned as I ran my hand up to her breast and I squeezed and sucked it, before I came down and kissed the slit of her cunt with my tongue. She gasped and exhaled. She was delicious!

Her eyes remained closed as she wanly smiled, satisfied, no doubt. Then, slowly she opened her eyes to sweetly gaze up at me before sitting up. I put my hand between her leg on her pussy once again stroking it. She made an attempt to speak, but I gave her no time, ramming my tongue into her gapping mouth kissing her mercilessly. She dropped upon the bed as I touched her cunt again. Running my tongue over her, I pushed it inside her. I couldn't get enough of her taste. She lay in ecstasy momentarily

I rose, pulling at my pants and walked over to the desk with my dick still hanging out of my slacks. A handsome man with black hair stared back at me from the mirror, a look of satisfaction displayed in his eyes. The naked beauty lay upon the bed, behind me. She sat up now, the shape of her nude body aroused me once more, and I was ready for round two. I tucked at my dick, stroked it and found it wet to the touch. It only excited me. Her nectar was all over me, soaking the very skin of the base and side of my legs.

"What have we done?" Something evil had awakened my beloved it. She looked lost once more, when she knew nothing of us. She wasn't that confused girl that didn't recognize us. That saw another reality, a sick one that would not allow us to connect.

I pushed back my hair and spun around. I made no attempts to zip my trousers. She rose from the bed and grabbed the robe off the floor, then quickly covered herself shamefully.

"What have we *done?*" She whispered furtively standing near the bed as I approach, still intoxicated. I needed to wake her from her hideous dream. The dream or, more apt, nightmare that separated us from one *another*. She began to cry. Why do you weep? I wanted to voice.

I rushed over and gripped a hold of her, grabbing at her hand and placed it on me. "We made love!" I exhaled pushing her to stroke me.

She panicked, struggling in my arms instead trying to pull away. There was a frozen, cursive guilt in her eyes. *You've been deceived*, I wanted to assure her.

"Take a hold of me," I pushed on. For a moment, she gripped my pecker and I delighted in the idea that she no longer feared our bond, our union. That, somehow, she had realized the deception was on us. She idly looked down at the floor.

"We made love, that's what we did! We belong together, my love." I moved upon her.

Her grip released my penis and I pushed into her forcing her waist to connect with mine. She exhaled deliriously as I kissed her neck, pushing her harder to me. *You need me just as I need you. I love you.*

She couldn't stop me, nor the overwhelming desire growing deep inside her. I felt it, just as I felt her warmth taking me in as I moved inside her with the passions of a demon, no... a devil.

It was right, everything, our love making. She belonged with me. She was mine...

"*No!* It's not right!" she cried, and pushed me back, pulling away and holding herself erect. She couldn't even look at me—she felt shame. But why? We were lovers in a far, far place; this was the dream. Why was she fighting these feelings?

"What have I done? Oh, *Nathan,* what have I done?"

I cringed at the sound of his name. As long as he was around, she would *never* see the truth. She would never feel it. The love, our love, our true love.

Sophia fell to the floor screaming as her body erupted into a massive tower of flames! I fell beside myself shaken with fear moving back, shocked at what I was seeing. My gentle and loving Sophia was covered in an endlessly unstoppable inferno, incinerating itself. I could do nothing to stop it. I felt helpless just as I felt every moment she wasn't in my arms.

IT WAS THEN I realized I was no longer standing in her bedroom. I was overlooking a deep pit, miles deep and more miles wide, filled with fire. I cried out, reaching for her into the loudly whipping rays, but she was gone, and the lifeless stump that had once been Sophia collapsed.

Below, I saw the ashen shape of her form scattering into an empty abyss.

"No... Sophia? *NooooOOOO!*"

6

THE STRANGE ENCOUNTER

SETH

I sat up and glanced around the room, recognizing the surroundings. It was a god-awful dream. I was in my office asleep the whole time? I leaned back in my seat and pushed back the ebony-black of my hair. The door of the office was closed. This was strange. I never closed my door, unless my darling Sophia was in the office, working with me.

I watched, the cool air of the office turning the hair of her skin upward, a chill ran up her slender arms, causing a ripple upon her sweet, tender flesh. It hardened her nipples beneath the thin, shapely dress she wore.

I'd gifted her a few lovely garments pleasing to my eyes, red being my most favorite color. Thin fabric, short and revealing. She wore them for me. She wouldn't deny that she loved them. Not to me.

Now, I thought of those moment as childish behavior. Is this what I did when I sought her attention? But when I began, I couldn't stop.

I could sit there, staring over at her, staring at her loveliness for hours, watching the hair on her arms rise, and deny herself she was uncomfortable.

The slit of her dress was slightly shorter. I fell into the routine and rhythm of observation. Her tits were nearly falling from within the open slit of the fabric, pouring like silk from the slender neck. Silky, milky, smooth and tender, well-rounded boobs.

My lap ached to have her on it, bent before me as I had many others do to satisfy my desires in the past. The body positioned forward, the backside facing me, my hands pushing back the fabric of the silk dress exposing the tender flesh of ass, my pants unzipped, my dick hard.

I licked my lips, pushing back my hair, grabbing at my pecker beneath the fabric. It was hard, just the idea, just the very thought, was making my dick push through the cloth of my pants.

I had women. Many pleased me, willingly on their ankles, lifting their miniskirts to tease and entertain me, but this was different.

I'd straddle them, punished them, pushed them upon my desk, my cock squeezed into their wet pussy. I gasped at the idea, it drove me mad and made me come repeatedly. Why did I always do this to myself? Their screams made me quiver; she would make me quiver far more, I had no doubt.

I curved a lip, adjusting my prick in my pants. I looked up, there was music in the distance. I hadn't realized what time it was. The weekend had officially begun, and I hadn't even recognized it. I rose and walked over to the window of my office, glancing down into the open dance floor. The dome was filled with people this evening, just like every other weekend. Nice-looking women, nice-looking men, none of which were truly worthy of me, none at all.

I was due for some companionship, I yearned for it, it called like a wicked banshee, my groin ached for pleasure and desire. On a prior night, I could have a group of ladies escort me into a motel and help me forget the one I deeply desired, but tonight, for some reason, I could not get her out of my head. She wasn't who she thought she was, what they thought she was. If she could only see that, discover what was right in front of her. What I had already realized myself. We were living a lie, and the truth was far simpler.

Now, no other woman would do. None of them could capture the divine essence, the supreme wonder of the being who she was in both life and death.

I dropped in my chair grabbing a hold of myself and thought of taking the frustration out, but one could not pleasure himself and be satisfied so easily. It wasn't enough; I wanted her. I needed the real pleasure of her firm body on my groin. I needed to satisfy the quench I could not silence. I dropped my face upon the desk, the desire was there. If I went to her and told her the truth of who we were, would she believe me?

Ramiel had denied I said a word. He had often said: *She must discover the truth herself. She must awaken. Rattle the gates and you will have chaos. You can lose her.* I slammed my fist upon the desk. It made no sense to hold back. I ached for desire, I longed for her embrace. If only she could see the truth. I wasn't who she— she was not—

That's all those little innocent eyes kept telling me, round like buttons popping as I unzipped my trousers longing to touch myself to silence the pain.

The observation realm, deepen, the *mirror* with devilishly patent delight. Oh yes, the looking glass, or what I called *The Mirror of Delicate Delights*. And rightfully so, a smirk curled my lip.

A look, a glance, to satisfy the curiosity of those wicked desires. The mirror had been secretly installed in the room next door to hers. It was placed in a reflection of accuracy to the dresser in her room, so it was like a window into her bedroom. My chambers were next to their room. I thought of being there now.

I had watched her before disrobing, reaching to touch the sylvan polished surface, so glaringly young and new that it shone, wishing it were her face, wishing it were her body. Only when the warmth of my semen fell over the top of my hand did I realize I had been just standing there the whole time, watching Sophia fucking Nathan.

I shook the thought far from my mind. I hated that man, hated the very sight of him, and the very idea that he was fucking the love of my life. It can't be. This was a cruel reality, one I could no longer face.

I rose once more, dragged myself to the window again, zipping my trousers as I did. My gaze fell over the nightclub crowd again; I saw Eric and the others by the bar, talking to some spectators. I watched Angelo doing his work and putting on a show like he always did, found the Elders taking pictures with some of the patrons. Perhaps I should start charging patrons for every picture those teeny boppers wanted. Everything and everyone was for sale, and if they were giving things away, I was losing.

I made a mental note of the incident, to discuss it later, I was due to meet with the group of misfits, set some ground rules. I had never officially conducted the meetings, Ramiel and Sophia arranged most things, and though I never attended, I thought I would be present at the next one.

I observed the patrons, witnessed a few getting tossed out for not following the rules. Saw others unable to enter. I witnessed women arguing with the security guy about getting past the ropes that led to my office. A sigh escaped my slim lips, unable to confront anything. And now, as I thought of her, I searched the dance floor for her.

I looked through the crowd of sweaty faces, and found where Eric sat. Eric, who happened to be sitting across the dance floor, facing my office. *That gothic freak!* Whose face was painted a ghostly white, a freak, a weirdo with false teeth, and long black hair, dressed in dark lace clothing. What was it all for, anyway?

I furrowed a brow, but Eric could not see me. Sophia wasn't with him, and I was happy of *that*.

I glanced over at the stage; the band had just ended their third song, I remembered hiring them to play for the weekend. They were a very popular group, not only locally but nearly everywhere. The lead singer's gothic appearance and music made him the most desirable on the list of those clamoring to get in. So, it wasn't hard to choose them.

I looked at the center of the crowd, and spotted a face, a figure that stood out. I thought I recognized the individual, but I wasn't sure. I took a better look; it was hard to see through the maze of people.

I peered closer, and then realized the figure was also staring back at me. *Can he see me through the special glass?* I wondered. I laughed, feeling foolish.

Of course not!

The individual began to move, walking up to the ropes separating the dance floor from the stairs, and stood perfectly still. I noticed he kept looking up, as though he knew I stood there. The figure was making me uneasy, but I didn't know why. Nothing made me uneasy. But he was. It was something about the way he was looking at me, like he knew I was up there. But how was it possible, when no one knew about the mirror window but those employed by the Cathedral?

I waited for the security guards to come and move the potential infiltrator away from the ropes, but none did. I swore I would make Ralph fire one or two of them, or worse.

The figure smiled up at me; his pale face was extremely familiar. His eyes were gray, almost white. His long, white hair draped over his handsome visage, and his smile was filled with both malice and a warning. He parted his lips, and from the folds of his mouth, long sharp canines- double ones- hung visible. No one would find him out of the ordinary, though. Of course, he fit right in; he was at the Cathedral De Los Vampiros.

I slowly backed away, and for some reason thoughts of Sophia concerned me. Had this *thing* read my mind? And how did I know or sense that he had? Was he about to do *exactly* what I feared of him?

"You stay away from her!" I yelled at the top of my lungs.

The quaint figure laughed as ample clouds of purple mist descended from its body; tentacles, like freakish arms of waste and horror, came out and surrounded him. The figure nimbly and simply leaped up onto the glass and through the window, where I stood.

Glass scattered and shattered everywhere, as the figure's body came through the window, splitting it into a million fragments.

———

I AWOKE, lurching from my bed in the midnight depths of utter darkness, sweat covering my body. Dazed, I looked around and realized I was in my bedroom. It was only a dream? *Or was it?* I wasn't sure any longer. The dream was always the same. Confusing; it was getting hard to distinguish any reality at all from the dreams.

It was silent in my room except for the faded music coming from a distance, where the dome sat in the Cathedral. Why had I gone to sleep so early on a Friday night? Then, I remembered Nathan was coming back tonight. Anything to avoid the old man...But then, I remembered the promise I had made to Sophia. A sigh left my open mouth. I fell back upon my bed. As I lay staring at the ceiling, I could not stop thinking of her, or the very image of her. It was like on many other such nights. At least I didn't have a painful erection over it like before.

I rubbed my tired face with one meaty paw, knowing what was surely to come. *Whatever* was stalking me, I vowed that it would not overtake me; not tonight.

7

CATHEDRAL DE LOS VAMPIROS

An individual must always live in his own world...

The local bars and clubs always seemed to die away if they were anywhere in the vicinity of the Cathedral de Los Vampiros. The Cathedral doors opened at ten on Fridays and Saturdays, and sometimes on special nights around the same time, except for Christmas.

The Cathedral steps descended way, way down before the patrons, as lines of people crowded the gigantic steps below the enormous building, where a long red carpet spread under their feet.

The lights came from behind the hugely looming structure and flashed from all around, making the building creepy and mysterious. A reddish glow lit up the area for several blocks.

Through its windows, the flashing of the lights shone, and with each time the doors were allowed open, hideously loud music poured out from its huge and monstrous chambers, to impress and bewilder those painted white faces outside the tall walls. Above the doors, a long black, red and white sign read: *Welcome to the Cathedral de Los Vampiros—Enter if You Dare!*

At the entrance, each night stood a man in black, and beside him a huge man wearing a muscle shirt, the label "Security" crossed his chest in red lettering. This man had shaven military-cut blonde hair, and a firm expression upon his broad face.

The other was a sickly, pale gentlemen dressed in black, who wore a top hat, with a cape waving behind him. His hair was long and black. He wore black trousers, a fancy, dark red vest, a white shirt underneath, and white gloves covering his hands in which he held a cane. His eyes were large and dark green, his face altogether bored, though clean with glittering white make-up.

His lips were thin, painted with black lipstick, and over his eyelids was a dark eye shadow that made his image even more ghostly. His nose was somewhat large, and a part of his forehead over-lapped his eyes like a frown. He was indeed a good-looking man, if you could see his sort of style as handsome.

An access pass was tied around his neck. Smiling, he revealed his canines to the crowd down below him, which seemed to cheer at him when he did so. He moved his cane over his hat to wave at them, as he stood upon a small platform. The bouncer standing next to him pushed his way to the front, to keep the crowd under control and away from the vampire.

As the pale man pointed the tip of his cane at those in the crowd surrounding him, the bouncers followed this instruction and allowed those he had chosen access into the Cathedral. It seemed no one would pass unless the vampire allowed it, and for now he only chose those most interesting to his gothic mood. Those in sport jackets, fancy dresses, or whatever else which didn't fit the vampire dress code of the Cathedral were ignored completely. Only a select few of the appropriate type were ever allowed in, a kind of pasty crème-de-lacrème of goths. Occasionally, non-gothic patrons were allowed in, but only a few.

Across the street, a strange mist hovered over the sidewalk, leaking from the sewers beneath and drifting up the alleys, unnoticed. An unseen force materialized, and the shape of man took form from the mist. It drifted up the stairs and vanished through the medieval doors and into the antechamber, passing spectators into the corridors beside the bar, where it disappeared underneath the employee's only entrance door.

Behind this door, an empty staircase led down into the vaults, where a variety of corridors and an entrance were hidden quite a distance from the party scene. Beyond that entrance, down the corridor were several hidden chambers. A sign above the door read: *The Sleeping Quarters of the Dead.*

Plastic toy torches with switches lined the way. The corridors were dim, gray-bricked walls with phony cobwebs on the corners. The corridors were wide enough for four people to walk side-by-side, and deep red carpeting lined the floors of the maze of chambers. As the directions split, there were several rooms closely built next to one another, which were decorated with coffin frames. Words in red painted over one door read: *Here Lies the Vampire Valentino.* There were several such signs, though they all very much read the same, one over each door.

At the end of the corridor there was a four-way cross, and hidden in the darkness with poor lighting, yet another door. The torches in this area were held in vampire skulls, and the doorknockers were vampire skulls with loops through their noses. The other doors were framed with tiny skulls, and on each door hung a clipboard with daily functions, assigned tasks and duties, plus meal schedules, deliveries, and inquiries concerning room service, specialties and daily activities concerning the Cathedral.

There were several other rooms that had been built separate from the rest of the chambers, but in the same location. There was a room with a heated swimming pool. The pool had access to a laundromat, which was located in the back, in a corner that led to yet another door. Another chamber was an entertainment room with a large television system and huge stereo speakers, four pool tables and a music system were inside. In the next corridor, in yet another room, was the cafeteria called *Bite,* with a long dining table and a number of expensive Victorian chairs. The entire interior had been decorated expensively and splendidly in Victorian Gothic.

The tables were set up with napkins, gothic silverware, and name places with the same names as the ones on the doors. The cafeteria was very large, with a television on the far corner mounted upon the brick wall. Nearby, two doors were placed- one leading outside the café and the other leading into the kitchen. The sound of the music suddenly surfaced again, the shouts of the crowd suffocated the dismal air, and the billowing smoke and the darkness concealed the misty form as it approached the top stairs.

The mist danced up the grand staircase; it crawled past the ropes and the oval-shaped office that laid empty, then into the corridor and up one more flight of steps. There was an eerie presence, a power and energy that announced it to the surrounding air. The walls seemed to bend, and then fall back into place as it passed. It once again took shape, and seemed to flicker in the shadows, remaining faceless. Two gray eyes sparkled within it, glowing from the darkness. The form began to guide down the corridor; any sound made its shape flicker slightly. It stopped at the end of the corridor, facing a closed door, and then it took a swift sniff of the air. A smile flashed in its glowing eyes, it vaporized, and the sparkling mist disappeared with a sucking sound underneath the door.

8

THE VISITOR

Strength, and strength gives life...

I walked from out of the bathroom of my bedroom, tying a tie around my neck. I stepped past the chair and grabbed my black suit coat. Just before I was about to walk out the door, I noticed the mirror window leading into Sophia's bedroom was open. Had I forgotten to close it? I had always reminded myself never to forget to close and conceal it. For if anyone ever found out its existence, I would have a lot of explaining to do. Not that it mattered to me; I needed a way of dealing with sexual perversion.

I walked back over to it, glancing briefly into the bedroom. Sophia was still lying on her bed, asleep. I had watched her undress and dropped in my own bed alone to satisfy the lust.

She stirred, the nightgown she wore shifted and revealed a portion of her naked breast. The excitement resurfaced through my veins, and I couldn't move away. Ideas began to stew inside my head. Everyone was downstairs, no one would come for hours. Or perhaps never come at all. I shouldn't, but there was no reason I could think of not to. What if she refused me? Or if she didn't believe me? What if she *didn't* want it, like I had been hoping she would? What *then?* I couldn't stomach the rejection, nor Nathan finding out what I had done, and separating us. No, I wouldn't let that happen. The possibilities, the insane ideas and my eternally horny dick kept reassuring me. N*obody* would hear her scream.

Dropping the suit coat on the chair, I smiled and unfastened the tie. Exiting the room, I walked towards the bedroom, putting a hand on the knob of the door. It wasn't locked, just as I figured. Sophia never locked the door.

Immediately, I entered, feeling myself hard almost instantly. Her figure lay on the mattress, undisturbed. I walked over to the side of the bed, and glanced down at her. The desire burned in my loins.

I resisted, trying to discourage my longings. This was insane. Walking out of the room, I scolded myself, but her slender form lying flat before me continued to mock me. Her tight, firm breasts poured from out of her gown, her exposed bare legs rang at me like an insistent phone call.

The gown laid open over one thigh, revealing her panties beneath. I grabbed at my growing strain, and took a seat on the mattress beside her. Slowly, I reached to touch her leg, running a hand up her panty line and slipping my fingers through her panties.

Sophia stirred slightly. I moved my hand away, but she didn't wake. I reached over again, my heart beating wildly in my chest, pounding so hard. I thought it would explode. I was afraid she would hear it. Again, I slipped my fingers into her, I felt her wet and warmth against the tip of my fingers. I wanted to drive them in deeper but instead stroked her pussy gently. She began to breathe heavily. Ah, you like that, my love. I gasped, aroused myself. I continued to stroke her gently before pulling away.

Carefully, I climbed on the bed over her, so that she lay beneath me. I towered over her, the lump in my groin growing and dying to breathe freely. I had made my mind up. I wouldn't be denied.

I pushed away all other doubts and the voices in my head that had previously haunted me.

I quickly put my hand over her eyes immediately she lurched up, but I forced her back down on the mattress, and pressed my lips against the back of her neck.

"Don't be afraid," I whispered, disguising my voice.

She was shaking beneath me, almost in tears, and her confusion seemed to have been replaced by fear.

"Who are you? What are you doing? Let me go!" she pleaded.

I took a breath, remained calm, and pressed against her, and whispered again into her ear.

"Just lay still. I'm not gonna hurt you."

She began to cry. I tried to silence her with gentle words, but she seemed to be aware of what was going to happen next.

"Please, don't do this!" she begged.

"Just be still. No one can hear you, so there's no point in fighting."

My hand slipped down her thigh, she trembled feeling my fingers against the warmth of her skin, then suddenly ripped her panties off. At once, she screamed, and I put a hand on her mouth.

"Just let it happen," I eagerly encouraged.

Sophia screamed and tried to fight me. She struggled in my arms. I didn't want her to see my face. I turned her face away from me, pressing her face deeply into the mattress. She was still screaming and crying, but now her cries were muffled.

"Sshhhhhhhhh!" I ground my teeth.

I reached down and unzipped my pants, pushing up against her, she screamed again, feeling the warmth of my dick on her backside. She fought me. Reluctantly, she fought me with every ounce of her being. *My darling,* I wanted to beg her. *Wake up!* I wanted to scream. *You love me; we love each other; wake up!*

I grabbed her arms and tied them against her back with a pillow-case, hitting her head on the backboard of the bed to silence her. Not realizing what I had done until she was still and silent. She had passed out.

I leaned forward, lifting her gown and spreading her legs apart. I pushed my fingers gently into her sex. The very feel of her juicy pussy was making me ejaculate. I curled up, exhaled brutally. My head was spinning as I pushed hard into her backside grabbing tightly at her bare ass, laughingly delightfully as I felt dizzy with excitement! My dick felt hard and hot pushing into her, the strokes were dry at first, forced going in, until the rapid sounds of my love making was all I could hear. Stroke after stroke, every inch of her I vowed to feel; hot and warm I pushed, biting down as each heated stroke made me want to release!

A sound from across the room, slowed my raps and I wrinkled my eyes over. The curtains fluttered and moved even. A form materialized from out of the darkness, darted forward spawning before me it knocked me off the side of the bed. I dropped with my dick in my hand and staggered to my feet to pull up my pants.

I looked about, but didn't see anyone as I stood in the bedroom holding up my pants. My cock was hanging out of my zipper. I raced to the curtains and pulled them apart, but there was no one there. I stepped away from the windows, glancing down at the mattress where Sophia lay sprawled. Dumbfounded for a moment as I came and reached for her. I wanted another taste; but so quickly a hand grabbed me and tossed me against the wall. I faced the attacker. It was the same eerie face from those dreams. It mocked me, as I released a snarl.

"You!"

I stumbled back against the wall trembling. The nightmare was coming to life.

"You stay away from her, you hear? Don't touch her!" I yelled, watching as it lingered near her bed.

The figure was dressed in a long cloak, with long, white hair that cascaded down his brawny shoulders. An eerie smile spread from cheek to cheek across his face. It glanced over at Sophia's figure upon the bed. It's face saddened as it reached a pale hand towards her. Immediately, I rushed forward at him. But with a lift of his hand, the mere gesture sent me back so hard I lost my balance and collapsed to the floor, weakened. Something strange was pushing hard upon me; I had no strength to rise or escape.

It neared her. What did it want with my beauty? I ground my teeth, fighting to rise and pull myself from of the ground.

The thing caressed gently at her face, as she lay unconscious. Spellbound, he touched her hair, and took in the sweetly cloying rose-petal scent of her. His fingers swept her soft skin, wiping the tears from her face. Her beauty glowed like white-hot coals, as it always had every time I saw her.

He wanted to kiss her, but didn't as he lay her down on the bed and draped the blanket to cover her.

I came from behind, stretching out a long wooden cane. The figure turned, and I at once drove it into him. The stranger screamed in agony; grabbing me angrily. I shoved him against the curtain and the window and drove the cane deeper into him. Pushing against him, I shoved him hard against the window using the other end of the cane. With all my strength, I rammed him against the glass. The window shattered with his weight, and he collapsed through it, disappearing over the ledge almost immediately.

I hesitated, but slowly walked over to the shattered window. The curtains were whipping in the strong currents of the wind. I glanced below, but saw nothing. Only a dark sidewalk and patrons looking back up at me from the streets. I ignored them and came closer to the edge of the window, searching the awning below fervently for any signs of a body, but there was nothing. *He surely must have died*, were my thoughts.

What had happened to the stranger? I looked across the side of the building, but found nothing. Stumbling away from the window, I ached both physically and sexually. I was unable to comprehend what had taken place, and was more afraid than puzzled.

At once, the door of the bedroom flew open and I quickly turned to zip my pants up as Ramiel and Nathan walked in. Alongside them, the vampire group also rushed in. I paid them no attention; still dazed, I had to get my story straight. I needed to explain my reasons for being here and for the shattered window. Nathan rushed to the bedside giving me a brief glance, but he was more concerned for Sophia. He dropped on the side of the bed trying to wake her, only looking back at me in search of an answer to what had occurred. However, I could give him nothing in that moment.

It was only seconds until Sophia regained consciousness; she sat up confused before a glimmer of realization merged in her eyes. At once, she embraced Nathan and began to spill her horrifying story in detail. The others crowded around the bed to listen. I stayed near catching certain details of the attack that had begun at my hands. I felt foolish and pained as I examined the hurt, I had caused her.

"Someone was in my room. Someone *attacked* me! I couldn't see his face. He covered my eyes!" She shook with piteous sobbing as she spoke, and Nathan tightly held her.

"He was going to rape me, Nathan, I didn't know what to do. All I remember is waking up with someone's hand over my eyes. He was on top of me, whispering, lying, saying no one would hear me!"

Santiago slammed his fist down on the bed frame angrily, the others seemed just as angry as he. I often wondered about his fascination with my mother, and I hated and despised him for having longings for her. It seemed everyone wanted a piece of her, including me.

The others were furious, looking at one another for answers. Children of nothing.

"I don't remember what happened after that. I passed out," she continued, sobbing once more.

Ramiel stepped over to me. He seemed keen to what had taken place. He was always aware no matter what, but it no longer surprised me. He was different in so many ways. Nathan glanced over at me just the same. I felt he was suspicious of me in some way. I listened to Sophia's story, remembering every single detail, but mostly what it felt to be inside her. I still tasted her sweetly bitter pyrrhic pelvic cunt. It was a victory.

"What transpired, Seth?" Nathan asked with that saddened pathetic expression of his fixed straight on me.

I glanced over at the old man. I hated everything about him down to his good looks, and those lovely blue eyes. He had nothing I wanted, except her.

"Did you see him? Did you see anything, son?" Nathan asked, holding back the tears. Sophia stood alongside him; I was immediately jealous.

The old man was enraged, having failed to protect Sophia. He blamed himself for the horrifying ordeal she had gone through.

I came to stand in front of the old man. Wiping the fingers I had harshly driven deeply into Sophia's pussy, I could still smell her lightly musky scent, and it was driving me mad with desire unable to keep my growing arousal hidden much longer.

"I did. I found the bastard on top of her, when I came to see if she needed anything. He tried to fight me, but I grabbed a prop cane, sitting in the corner and drove it into him! I killed him!"

A smile from both Santiago and Valentino flashed proudly and I realized it was their prop cane that I had used against that stranger.

"We struggled briefly; that's when I pushed him against the window and he fell through," I continued.

Ramiel moved over to the window sneaking a look, the others did the same, glancing down below over the ledge. But just like I, they could not find the body. It was quite a drop from the second floor. Their faces questioned, *If Seth said he threw him out the window, where was the body?* I wondered that myself. It was starting to dawn on me this was no ordinary intruder, but something Ramiel had warned me about should I push Sophia to me far too quickly.

"Seth, are you sure you threw him out the window?" Ramiel questioned, turning to meet my eyes. I furrowed a brow. How could he even ask such a question, standing in front of a window that looked like a bus had driven through it?

"How can you ask me that...after seeing that?" I pointed toward the window, but it was a good question. The missing body undoubtedly would arise questions if someone had been shoved through it.

"Shouldn't there be a *body?*"

The others wanted to ask the same question, I could see it in their eyes, fortunately for them it was Ramiel who did, for they didn't dare. Instead, they glanced back at Ramiel hoping he would get to the bottom of it. Sophia immediately came over and hugged me; it caught me off guard. I would have thought she had fallen from the fantasy of this world and was ready to receive me as her lover, but it was merely wishful thinking.

"Thank you, darling, for being there when I needed you," she whispered into my ear, nearly weakening me. It took all my strength to keep myself from falling over. She pulled away back into Nathan's arms. I bit hard down at my lower lip, with agonizing jealousy.

"Technically, yes," I said regarding Ramiel's question. "That's the same thought I had, when I first glanced down, and didn't see one."

"*What?* Could he have survived?" Nathan asked concerned.

"I seriously doubt that, Nate," Ramiel answered, chuckling slightly. However, it was a perfectly good question, I knew Ramiel would answer. He knew just as I knew something wasn't right here. He shot me a glance the others missed.

"I am sorry, Sophia. I know, I'm supposed to protect you. I'm sorry I wasn't here to do so." His gray eyes sadly glance over at her.

"Don't be so hard on yourself, Ramiel. It wasn't your fault. Besides, Seth saved me." She reached for my hand. It sent a chilling sensation up my arm. It was happening more often. And it was hard to contain.

A difficult smile appeared on my face, and I felt horrible almost immediately. The group of misfits rewarded me with appraisals of a job well done. And even tentatively I accepted an embrace from Nathan.

"You did well, *Son,*" Nathan said, patting my shoulder in a fatherly manner.

The others left the room, leaving Sophia and Nathan with

Ramiel and I. As soon as they were gone, and when Nathan and Sophia were preoccupied, Ramiel pulled me to one side, pushing me along to walk towards the doorway. I reluctantly followed, curious as to what had occurred. I had a feeling he was going to say something in regard to that. I was growing restless when I glanced back and caught Sophia kissing Nathan. I wasn't even listening when Ramiel started talking. He slapped the side of my arm, I flinched far more irritated with the distraction.

Slightly dazed, I glanced over at him furrowing a brow. I gave him a snarl.

"What exactly occurred here?" Ramiel asked. He was no fool, and I knew that. He was waiting for the truth from me.

"Exactly what I said," I tried to say, unable to say further fearing I would be heard. I shot him a grimace. "Do you *doubt* me?" I pushed, toying with him. I knew it was a foolish thing to do. Since he could easily know what had happened. In fact, I didn't doubt he already did.

"You know I already know. Why do you find it necessary to deny it or hide it from me? What did you do? " Ramiel asked, as I slowly met his eyes. Guilt was very notable in my eyes; I couldn't hide the truth of the horrible things I had done.

He pulled me closer and away far from the entrance.

"You attacked her," he whispered. "I warned you," he continued while pulling me away into the hallway a distance from the doorway.

I glanced back into the room.

"It's getting hard, Ramiel. I can't fight what I feel. I can't...I want to be with her," I whispered, nearing.

He cupped my cheek immediately as I stood facing him, desperately looking for sympathy from him.

"Give it time, Seth," he offered. "You can't rush things, not destiny."

I groaned, angry at his words.

"I can see your pain; I completely understand it, but this is a dangerous game. We don't want to fail."

"Understand? Fail?" I growled.

"One can't rush destiny, my boy. It will be. I foresee it."

"Fuck destiny," I boldly snapped, trying to keep my voice down. "How can you say that after what happened, Ramiel? It's here. The one thing you warned me about. That was no ordinary person who attacked her. It was *him!"*

Ramiel put a hand on my shoulder, pulling me closer to keep me from attracting the attention of Sophia and Nathan.

"That's what I wanted to speak to you about, Seth. Tell me. We must talk about this." Ramiel's eyes were glowing brightly.

I had known Ramiel for a long time now. As the story went, Ramiel had brought my Sophia and Nathan together before I came to this world. He had, in a sense, prepared this world for me. He had been the original owner of the Cathedral, and my guide to all the dreams and fantasies that followed thereafter, drawing me closer to my destiny, as he claimed.

Ramiel knew about my obsession. He knew who I really was. He was aware of my feelings long before even I was. As a matter of a fact, Ramiel had encouraged them. He understood my emotions and my heightened reactions to Sophia. Of course, at first, I had doubted his motives, afraid he would reveal my growing desires to Sophia or Nathan, but soon after I became his devoted disciple. Crazy as my desires may have been, I trusted Ramiel to make it a reality.

———

"You want her, only because you *know* she belongs with you." Ramiel had told me once. "You love her, because she's your love. Your feelings are not wrong and have always been the one thing to guide you," Ramiel said. "She's not your mother. And you are not her son. This is the illusion, the cruel illusion to set you apart. The illusion that was placed by a force to keep you from the woman you love. You were lovers *before* in another time."

He revealed far more about my reincarnation, of a life previous to this one. I was at awe with the discovery. Things began to make sense, my feelings, my longings. I was not this fiend, this pervert. An illusion, Ramiel had revealed. A wicked ugly illusion set by forces that wanted to control me and keep me away from my love.

Had Ramiel spoon-fed the same inappropriate lie that Nathan would accept? Wasn't that what Sophia believed? Yet what *had* Ramiel referred to Nathan as being? A vessel, a tool of divine power —*whose* divine power?

Was he referring to me?

But I hadn't come to understand fully who I was, Ramiel revealed with time I would know the extent of my being. The dreams made sense, rather than the life I now was living. Until then, Ramiel was my only guide. The way that I saw the fantasy and the reality were completely distorted.

"We must talk about *him* seriously," Ramiel whispered, but my attention seemed to be elsewhere,

as I watched Sophia taking a few items from her dresser, as Nathan helped her pack a small suitcase.

I moved into the room leaving Ramiel outside in the hall looking after me.

"What's going on?" I foolishly asked; this would surely ruin my peep shows.

"I'm moving your mother to the bedroom downstairs. She can't stay in this place. It's not safe for her up here. Eric and the vamps downstairs can keep an eye on things."

I would have argued with the old man, bashed his face in if allowed. I was here, there was no need for such a thing. I could protect her. *Hadn't I?*

"But I'm here, Fath—father." I bit at my lip, forcing the word father from my mouth. Ramiel shot me a glance.

"I know, sweetheart, but I don't want to be here. Understand that. I just don't feel safe, not now at least," Sophia said.

"Besides, this place is a mess—it's for the best," Nathan interrupted, stepping forward.

I trembled, as she neared and cupped my face. She seemed troubled. I was a fiend for having scared her. Her gestured seemed to want to prevent an argument between Nathan and me, if I didn't know her any better. I eased as her small, delicate hand stroked my cheek. It was hard to resist or hide the mounting erection.

As fastest as she had taken my cheek into her palm, she left me turning back to Nathan and kissed him. And I knew they would be making love later that night.

I stormed from the room walking out the bedroom into the hallway, forgetting Ramiel was beside me. Ramiel stepped alongside me and pulled me with him.

"Relax, and come with me," the wiser older man said. *"Now."* He demanded when I resisted.

I wanted to tell him to fuck off and take his fortune telling-ass elsewhere, but I didn't. I trusted him, and I knew he would give me the answers I needed. So instead, I eagerly followed.

9

SOPHIA'S DREAM

I lay on the bed, trying to close my eyes and sleep. A cold breeze blew into the room; and I curled up, spreading my legs slightly. I heard a voice calling to me with a soft and comforting lilt to it. The name whispered was different, meaningless to my soul, yet I recognized it.

Suddenly, I found myself in a garden, surrounded by millions of beautiful, red roses. The petals were covered by drops of water, and a summer shower had lifted their scent into the air. I danced among the roses, gliding on a cloud of mist. The voice grew closer as I glanced about racing in slow motion through the roses, feeling their thorns clutch at and rip at my legs.

I heard the voice approaching, but I couldn't see anyone. The name was familiar the voice sounded like a song so soft. I recognized it, but didn't know why.

I continued through the rose path, and in the distance, I saw a figure, but I couldn't make out the face. It was blurry and seemed almost unreal. I hurried, as the thorns of roses ripped at my gown and pulled it apart, but that didn't stop me. Pieces of the gown slipped across my body, some dangling against my bare skin, a few torn completely until a portion of my body was exposed and bare. My nakedness didn't bother me. I felt free and alive, running bare against the breeze with the fabric barely sticking to my body. With each step, the image in the distance came closer, but seemed to refuse to reveal himself.

I stopped, the figure had vanished. All I saw were roses everywhere I looked and an endlessly beautiful blue sky above me.

A whisper spun me around, and I found myself face-to-face with the figure in a black cloak.

I felt a strange attraction and I didn't know why. Yet, I wasn't afraid.

I heard the voice again, coming from every direction, whispering a name I knew as I gazed desperately into the dark hood, trying to see a face behind the starry sheets of darkness.

I came forward and reached over slowly. Did I dare lift the hood from the form? Beneath it, a handsome man's face framed with long, white hair and beautiful dark features gazed back at me.

His almond eyes beckoned to me. Strangely, I felt safe. There was something mysterious about him.

The figure took hold of my hands suddenly. I didn't pull away as we began to spin. Intoxicated, I fell in his arms. The remaining threats of my gown fell away from my body. I felt his hands on me, as a strange control came over me, feeling a peace I hadn't felt before. I felt drawn to him, felt his presence and his lips kiss my neck as I tossed my head back. I quivered in his arms, quivered at his touch, feeling the energy running inside me and racing all over my body, sending chills down my spine. A flutter exploded inside my belly. I felt foolish for falling so easily, but I couldn't help it any longer. I beckoned him to me. I fell back among the roses, felt the thorns prick my skin as he came over me, and spread apart my legs in his descent. He silently lowered himself to me, his lips parting as he pressed them hungrily against my mouth. I begged him to me again, I wanted him. I didn't understand why the desires were so great; I couldn't contain them any longer. I was a prisoner of my own lust, I was gone.

I felt the hard-dry of his pecker push inside me. I exploded with delight and longing. I bit at my lower lip in agony as he lowered and pushed with all his might deep inside me!

"Yes!" I moaned deliriously. I ached to feel it. The agony and hunger of my sex ached, washing and drenching my pussy. The pink of my nipples was pricked hard, as my excitement grew and with his every thrust, I gasped in sheer delight, feeling his body pounding me repeatedly.

I wanted more; I didn't want it to end. The handsome lover gazed into my eyes; somehow, he resembled Nathan and it excited me more. The change had been strange and so abrupt. There was something different in him. A power I couldn't resist. I pressed him close, grabbed at his buttocks as his thrust quickened.

I felt his breath against my neck, his chest grazed the hardness of my nipples. I moaned again, groaned and whimpered in musical delight. I was overcome with the desire moving along with him.

His voiced suddenly whispered softly. I hadn't heard him at first. A hard, painful thrust sent me into an explosive sensation and ecstasy. I gasped and finally came to the moment of orgasmic climax.

"Don't be afraid."

I froze. His thrust didn't end as I felt every single delightful sensation of his penis moving inside me.

"I'm not gonna hurt you. Just let it happen."

I wrinkled my nose quizzically at those familiar words.

Then, I knew.

Seth facelifted over me, his thrusts continued as his eyes flared wildly and his mouth dropped into a gap of sheer agonizing pleasure. I didn't know what to do. He rammed harder, he seemed mad. I tried to push him off, but he wouldn't get off or let me go. Why did I resist? He wondered. Something in me was giving way. Something in me wanted to let go and press him close. Why was I afraid? That small voice wondered. "This isn't right," the other half was saying. What is right? An unusual verse fell from his gorgeous mouth.

"This is us. We are meant to be together. You feel it," he hissed.

I shook my head.

"No, this is wrong. This is a dream, a hideous nightmare."

His thrusts became harder, pounding against my pelvis so hard it hurt when they connected with my torso. Strangely, my struggles seemed feeble, and the fight seemed to die inside me.

I moaned, feeling the orgasm overcome me, I felt ashamed and yet a release I had long to feel. "Yes, that's it!" I heard his voice say. "Accept it, my love. This is us."

Sweat draped my brow as I exploded. Seth dropped hard upon me crying out in orgasmic delight.

"Yes, yes!" I gripped hold of his buttocks, that rocked him far more and he quivered in my arms. I felt shame almost immediately that my desires had overcome me. What was happening to me?

"You're awakening," he whispered as I felt his breath against the lower part of my neck, kissing me.

I couldn't contain my arousal within that moment.

"This is who we are. We are not a mother and son, that is the illusion. Remember, we are lovers." Still, I resisted pushing him back. He didn't move. My attempts were feeble and useless as I struggled to escape a feeling that had a hold of me far too much.

"Don't fight it," Seth hissed. I didn't want to any longer or resist the prick of his groin thrusting continuously into me. I moaned and whimpered once more until I was overcome, and I could no longer break away. I just couldn't. I exhaled moaning so loudly...

I awoke and sat up covered in sweat. Blushing highlighted the pale of my cheeks as I felt a wetness between my inner thighs. Embarrassed, I rose finding Nathan asleep alongside me. He didn't move.

Carefully, I stumbled towards the bathroom. Closing the door behind me, I thought of Seth, and his peculiar behavior, but what had caused such strange and taboo dreams? The dreams were one thing, but feeling arousal and desire were another. My body quivered, I was shaking; my legs trembled and my sex ached both with excitement and his painful thrusts.

I reached down to touch my aching cunt; my hand came away soaked. My whole lower body was throbbing with pleasure, I was ashamed. What was happening to me? Why was I feeling this? For my...I shook my head. This was all wrong. The dreams... The feelings... The sexual desire and longings... They were misplaced. I felt a hunger unlike I had before in that dream.

I had a hard time standing, my legs were trembling, and my body ached. I pressed and grabbed my breasts feeling their tender soreness and exhaled recalling the dream. I pressed the pink hard point of my nipples between my fingers. I bit my lips, falling into that vision of his body pressing over mine and pushing upon my tits. It was agonizing trying to forget, I couldn't. I caught my reflection in the mirror. It revealed a partially white gown barely covering my frame, falling over my shoulder, and visible bruises from my rough sexual encounter. What would I tell Nathan? I no longer cared; at least, that wild part of me didn't at that moment.

I wanted his lips on me again, any part of me. I shook my head, but the images of that dream wouldn't allow me to forget. His rough hands running against my skin, his hard cock ramming inside, me. I ached no matter how hard I wanted to deny it. I longed for it.

"Stop this," I whispered. "It was a nightmare, a dream."

But I couldn't. I thought of his words, those that he had repeated to me in that moment of hard sex. *This is the illusion; we are not mother and son. We are lovers. Remember...we are lovers.* What did that mean? Was I using that as justification for what I wanted?

*We are lovers...*Why did I feel there was some truth to those words as crazy and disturbing as they were?

10

THE MEETING

ERIC

Strive, reach, and take. Then you shall not be taken.

On this particular evening, we sat in the oval-shaped office waiting for Ramiel, having been given permission to use it. There had been a large, coffee-brown meeting table within the office no one other than Seth had used to spread his paperwork on. Ralph and the other bouncers brought in a large box. I watched them as they set up on top of the table.

My hands were shaking as I came to arrange all the items we would need for our meeting while gazing at the box with some curiosity. I wondered what it could be. It was sealed. The others all came in and took their seats.

It was odd to find myself in this office once more but without Seth in it to disrupt or cause tension. Where was he this evening? After our meeting, I was afraid to see him again. I could feel my heart pounding within my chest and the blood in my veins racing whenever I even thought about him. No wonder my hands were shaking. A warm hand took me and I spun my head back to find Sophia smiling at me.

"You okay?" she asked. I smiled, happy to see her bright brown eyes looking at me.

I nodded, then looked over at the box. She followed my eyes and grinned.

"What's in the box?" I asked.

She smiled. "You'll soon find out." And with that, she moved away.

I thought about her work. In fact, I still remembered her typing away in her room, the words soaring inside her head and her lips twisted in a little as she was determined to finish her piece.

She had been working so hard for so many years.

Sophia's large brown eyes sparkled with golden hues rich in color, so beautifully alive we were caught in their magical dance.

Dressed in a long, red satin dress, her dark hair came down over her shoulders. She was the most beautiful thing I had ever laid eyes on. She was a beauty I thought could only be a dream, or a character in a well-written novel.

"I have great news, everyone." She rose; I hadn't even been made aware of this great news. I was usually the one by her side, the all-powerful and knowing Eric. Her right-hand man when Nathan wasn't there. I was proud of that title. And I made it known.

"What is it, Sophia?" The others looked up with their pasty faces and parted lips where there hung fake fangs, entranced by her every word, their eyes went wide. They appeared startled, trying to find an answer among each other, but there was nothing but confusion surrounding the table in the small interior office this evening.

What was this great announcement?

Then, as if in queue, Nathan entered the office. Everyone was surprised to see him. No one knew he was still here, most of the time he didn't stay long. Always away on business, it was startling to see him. He was a tall form of a man dressed in a clean dark navy suit, handsome, with dark coarse hair and bright, bold, green eyes. He was a beauty just as Sophia. Nathan had always been the more silent of the two. A statue of a god, who worshiped his goddess in silence. A bold man that, if needed, could voice his own opinion in a frightening, yet, respectable manner. He was kind, but unlike Sophia, he was not one to indulge in the world she had created in her works nor in the great cathedral she had inherited from their adopted father. He was more of a silent investor.

At times, I felt he wanted to take her away from all this and romance her and emerge her into his world. His job took him around the world, and away from her quite often. It was something that I knew he hated. I couldn't say what Nathan did for a living, but at times he would be gone for weeks and sometimes, it would be a month before he returned. Whatever he did took a lot of his time.

WHEN HE ENTERED, Nathan carried a large box in his hands. Another box? He dropped it upon the meeting table in the office. Sophia had been using his office to write and hold group meeting regarding the cathedral duties. I helped, but there was always so much to do, it often gave Sophia no time to do what she adored, and that was writing.

Nathan immediately embraced Sophia planting a kiss on her lips. There was a single moment between them where they seemed far away until I cleared my throat. Sophia blushed, and Nathan, well, did what Nathan does; he smiled in that handsome manner.

He moved toward the box. Sophia leaned next to him and he pulled her close.

"Shall we tell them?" Nathan teased stroking his wife's cheek tenderly.

I rose from my seat and neared the table, where all the others were glaring back at the both of them wide-eyed, unable to speak.

Their faces still hung with the question, what was the announcement?

I looked at Sophia in the same manner, constantly gazing and zooming down at the box on the table, with a single questioning stare. Sophia had been writing for so long a series of novels. Could this be what I thought it was? Was it the finished product?

I wondered what Ramiel would say. Where had he been this morning? I wasn't sure why the thought crossed my mind suddenly. He never lasted for more than a day before he was gone again.

And as quickly as I had wondered, Ramiel appeared. Two titans in the same room. After last night I sensed that's why Ramiel had remained. There could be no other reason. It seemed Sophia, and even Nathan, looked surprised to see him. Had they thought the same? Had they been wondering why he was still around?

"Ramiel?" Nathan asked. His voice sounded disappointed; he appeared far more surprised than all of us. Sophia, on the other hand, came to Ramiel's side and embraced him.

"I would have thought you'd be long gone by now."

Ramiel wrinkled his nose. I felt that in some manner Nathan had insulted him by the way he furrowed a brow back over.

"After Sophia's eventful night, I wouldn't dream of leaving. At least, not yet." He neared.

Ramiel was tall with white locks of hair, and although he appeared far older, there was a beauty I found in him that I had not seen in others. He wore a black suit with a red tie. His piercing blue eyes flashed over at us as he took Sophia into his arms, pulling her back, he stroked a lock of her hair and kissed her forehead. He was like a father to both of them, but far more to Sophia. She was his adopted daughter.

I did not know the details of their story, but I knew enough to know she had come first, and then it had been Nathan. It seemed Ramiel had brought them together, and strangely, now seemed to be the driving force that was trying to pull them apart. Whenever he was around, he seemed to come between the two of them.

There seemed to be tension in the room whenever he was present between him and Nathan. Were Ramiel's demeanor and the way he enjoyed controlling things when he was here putting the other man off? It seemed to bother Nathan far more this evening. No one had been as close to Sophia as Ramiel.

Ramiel looked at the group and at the boxes sitting at the desk. "Have I interrupted something?" he said, but the way he made it sound, it was clear he was very much aware that he had. His news, if any, was far more important than our little gathering. That was clear as he made no attempt to allow us to continue.

Sophia smiled and seemed to be the only one to doing so. I felt what Nathan felt, utter irritation at the tone of Ramiel's words. He neared his wife, who stood between the two men. They seemed to be in competition for her affection and attention.

"Ramiel, I didn't know you were planning on staying. I'm so happy," Sophia said, gazing happily over at him. She seemed the happiest to see him.

"Of course, my darling, after what you experienced I couldn't bear to leave unexpectedly." Recalling the event only saddened her. He put an arm around her shoulder to comfort her.

The fact was, Ramiel hardly made an appearance or a visit to the cathedral, and rarely did he stay for long. The only time he appeared was if he had news about something of great importance. If it wasn't for Sophia's great announcement, then what? Perhaps it was as he had said, concern. It appeared Nathan wondered the same while staring over at him, slightly annoyed. It made me question why he often allowed it.

"We were just about to unveil Sophia's great achievement," he interrupted, not allowing Ramiel to voice his reasons for his unannounced appearance.

The tall, older gentlemen grimaced while standing even closer to Sophia. He put his arm around her shoulder and pulled her close. Nathan had to adjust his own arm to avoid his. He pulled away before his arm came into contact with that of the club owners'. Sophia suddenly looked uncomfortable between the two.

"Nathan, I thought you were on your way to New York? I must admit, I was rather surprised to see you here myself."

Nathan gave Ramiel a queer look; it made me feel uncomfortable for him. The tone in Ramiel's voice sounded annoyed and arrogant by Nathan's interruption, and far more by his presence.

"I don't leave until later tonight," Nathan immediately answered. "Besides, I wanted to be here for my wife's announcement. This is a great achievement for her. And I'm very proud of her," he boosted.

Sophia looked over at him, leaving Ramiel's side. She wrapped her arms around Nathan, and for a moment, they seemed lost in each other's gazes. It was when Nathan leaned forward to kiss her that Ramiel began to speak again. Disrupting their lovely kiss for his own selfish news. He was far more interceptive this evening than any other.

"I'm sorry, my dear, I forgot. I didn't mean to intrude on your happy celebration—you know I've always been proud of you."

Sophia glanced over at him. She smiled and the sparkle in her eyes seemed to regard him kindly.

"You didn't intrude," she answered staring over at him.

"Let's have a look," he immediately said. Ramiel reached over and pulled open the box before Nathan could object. He lifted a series of books from within. It appeared as if Nathan had wanted to let his wife do the honors, but once more Ramiel had come between that.

"You did it!" he said proudly staring at the books in his hands. "You finished all of them?" Nathan was silent as Ramiel laid the books on the table and displayed them for the others to see.

Sophia smiled back at all of us, but soon after, her eyes begged for a remark from our shocked faces.

"Well... Anyone?" Ramiel voiced at our silence.

The others' voices broke out delighted by the news of Sophia's great accomplishment.

"Sophia, that's awesome! You finally did it!" Damien exclaimed and rose to break the long silence. She embraced Sophia. I was delighted, of course; it was wonderful news. A great accomplishment. At the other end, Nathan's utter silence and Ramiel's queer behavior had me distracted. I had seen it before, but for a strange reason he seemed far colder this evening.

The others came to congratulate Sophia. Then, it was the elders turn. Santiago and Valentino stepped up to her.

Valentino reached forward and hugged her; Sophia seemed surprised by the gesture. The elders were never to affectionate with others, much less friendly, but this was Sophia.

Then, it was Santiago's turn. He was wary this evening, though, gazing over in Nathan's direction. The man of the house was aware of his affection for his wife and his eyes watched the elder carefully and threateningly. It made him somewhat less confrontational and flirty with Sophia, but no less daring.

He bowed to her taking her hand and kissed it. "Congratulations, my dear lady," he politely said.

I furrowed a brow over at him, moving my head sideways to remind him of Nathan's presence at the other end of the room. Why did he have to be so direct? Did he think that Sophia was just gonna drop into his hands? He needed to show our boss some respect.

I noticed at the other end of the room Nathan and Ramiel were talking, but I couldn't hear what was being said. The group had moved to the center of the office. Their voice seemed to be growing. I wondered if they were arguing.

Santiago turned and glared directly at me.

"I always knew you would succeed. You're so talented." Santiago was polite to say. "Nathan must be so proud. Such talent and such beauty. How can one have any self-control in the presence of such a lovely lady?"

And on that note, he slowly wandered away.

"Well, gather around now, children, I bring news," Ramiel suddenly voiced, from the other end of the office. He had stepped from the front of the office over to us. *Children?* My face and those of my companions seemed to question his choice of words.

We took our places, all seated speechlessly erect in our assigned seats. Because many fights came out of who would sit where to discontinue any further arguments we were given a specific sitting place.

He looked over at Sophia. Nathan approached from behind him. Moving to his wife, he reached for her hand, which Ramiel took instead pulling her close.

"I'm pleased to announce that Seth will be joining us this evening."

Nathan looked ready to object, but a knock interrupted him, and we all looked towards the door. The door opened and the first person who entered was our security intel, Ralph. Our security was a larger man, not by weight, but by upper muscle. He had been a bouncer and wrestler in his previous life.

"Ah," Ramiel gleamed. "And here he is, just in time."

Ramiel seemed cold-hearted at the idea of Nathan's departure. Did he not care what affect it had on poor Sophia?

Nathan looked over at him, but he was quiet in voicing his dislikes of the man Sophia seemed to respect. I wished that he had. The man could be such a brute.

"I guess that's for me," he said as Ralph waited for him by the door.

Sophia went into his arms and they embraced with Ramiel looking on as if their display of affection bothered him.

"I'm so proud of you," Nathan whispered to her. She smiled as he kissed her head. Nathan cupped his wife's cheek, glanced over at his mentor, Ramiel, and nudged his head.

"Have a good trip, Nathan. Don't worry about Sophia. I'll take good care of her while you're gone," He said to the young lord. But it was in the manner that he said it that made my nerves tense and troubled.

Nathan pressed his lips together and nodded. He kissed Sophia once more and disappeared through the office doorway.

AFTER HE WAS GONE, we waited patiently, yet were growing nervous. We were hoping that we wouldn't see Seth this evening, gracing us with his presence.

Sophia took her seat. She seemed troubled; her eyes were cast down facing the table. Ramiel was standing by the mirror window of the office looking down into the foyer? I wondered if he was looking at Nathan leaving. Was he making sure the man was gone?

Damien found her silence troubling, and she was worried. She signaled over to me from the other end of the table to say something. I shook my head; I didn't want to. Damien nudged me again. I rolled my eyes and finally pushed myself to speak.

"Sophia, are you okay?"

She blinked; noticing everyone staring in her direction, and smiled. Or, at least, she seemed to put a smile on her face.

"I'm just a little tired. I didn't get much sleep after last night," she said.

Damien shook her head over at me for asking. Seriously hadn't they told me to ask?

"I just miss him," she admitted regarding Nathan. "I wish he didn't have to leave any more. I wish..."

I felt foolish for asking.

I was such an idiot for listening to them.

"Great move, Eric. Can't you see she had a bad experience?" Valentino sternly said.

The elders furrowed their eyes in my direction. I ignored Santiago's and Valentino's voices at the other end of the table. Angelo told them both to shut up, with a forcible wave of his hand. Sophia seemed a little troubled by the immensity it was causing everyone.

"It's alright," Sophia made herself say, in my defense. "Thank you for your concern, Eric."

The room became silent and Sophia took a breath. She seemed miserable and uncertain about something. Having Nathan around gave her strength, but now she seemed drawn into what troubles lurked in her mind.

"If you want to talk about it, I'm here for you, we all are." I smiled, as the others, including Santiago and Valentino, declared the same.

Sophia's shy eyes met mine.

"I know, thank you, all off you...."

RAMIEL RETURNED to the center where the table sat. He looked confident and delighted while unbuttoning his suit. He took his seat on the large wooden seat beside Sophia and leaned back in his chair to relax.

I rose from my place and walked over to the table in the back of the office where a tray of glasses had been arranged on a rolling table for us. There was coffee and a pitcher of iced tea, condiments were set aside as well. A set of desserts were arranged in a serving dish: pastries, Danishes, and other delicious delights.

I poured some coffee into a large mug, looking around the back office at the family pictures set upon the bookshelf. I glanced back toward Sophia silently sitting beside the arrogant form of our boss, Ramiel. He was telling her something, but I couldn't hear what. Their conversation seemed to be a private one. I worried about her.

I took the cup and condiments and set them beside Ramiel. He immediately turned his attention towards me. I hadn't meant to drop them on the table so boldly, but I wanted his attention diverted from Sophia. She seemed a bit uncomfortable.

It was only when his eyes met mine that I regretted it. He was tapping a nail on the table and narrowed his eyes at the coffee beside his hand.

"Is this for me?" he curiously grinned, I saw two double canines stick out from between his red stained lips.

"Yes, sir," I said, biting at my lip.

The smile on his face spread wider.

"Just like you like it, sir, black." He looked down into the mug quickly.

"Appreciate it," he simply said. He had gotten far more arrogant. The more he was away, the more he seemed a distance from his older self. One time in our lives, we had known a different man. A kinder, and sweeter, less fearsome person than the one that now was presenting himself to us.

The others were just gazing in our direction. I wasn't the only one that felt his change. At one time, we had seen him as a father figure, worshiped him to some extent, but now we only feared him and were afraid of what else he was capable of. What else didn't we know about him? He held all the cards, he wanted us gone. What could stop him from making it happen?

I MOVED AWAY with him looking on. His eyes said 'go away boy' as he took the mug and drank. I noticed that Damien had taken the seat beside Sophia. I gave her a glance in which she motioned me away, like shooing a fly.

She stuck her tongue out at me and anyone else who would protest her position.

Finally, I gathered their attention by pounding loudly on the table. I stood at the front of the table away from the door. Santiago frowned over at me, and once both he and Valentino gave me the sign of the cross, which meant death for our kind.

I ignored them and continued, but their every movement seemed to be crying out to me. I couldn't help losing my place, and sometimes, I fumbled through the pages of my material. It was frustrating. I wasn't much in giving presentations, let alone a speech to my employers, who were sitting and waiting to hear what plans we had to enhance the Cathedral, and what requests we could offer them considering our quarters.

Ramiel placed his cup down on the table, listening politely. It was more than I could ask for.

I was dressed in a velvet red robe, a gift from Sophia.

She said I wore it well. Underneath it, I sported a vest with a ruffled shirt, the cuffs of which sprouted from under the sleeves that hooded my hands. My slacks were black, and my vest was a ruby velvet color with golden filigrees at the edges. Though I never wore a tie, I used the only black one I owned that evening. My long ebony hair hung loosely and neatly over my broad shoulders as I held up my notebook and began reading off the names on the page.

Everybody came to order at the call of their names, with the exception of Valentino and Santiago. They simply glared over at me, as if to say we're here, duh. I didn't say a word in return, no doubt they were.

"Are we starting?" Ramiel asked, sitting himself defensively back, and then gazing over at Sophia.

"Yes, sir..." I managed to answer in a shaky voice. The others looked at me, then at Ramiel.

"You are aware we are still waiting on Seth? Have I not made that clear? He is joining us this evening."

I swallowed what I wanted to say.

I placed the notebook down on the table, as the room grew uncomfortably silent. I thought no one would bring up Seth, but I should have known the only one to do so would be Ramiel. Was I that naive? Why wouldn't he?

"He *was?*" Sophia asked, glancing over at Ramiel. Of course, she knew, hadn't Ramiel announced it before coming into the meeting?

She was nervously stirring in her seat, unable to directly look Ramiel in the eyes.

"Yes, he is, my dear," he immediately responded, a modicum of sarcasm in his tone.

"I'm surprised he's not here. It's not like him. Perhaps something came up. I'm sure it must be important for him to be...*late.*"

"Perhaps," Sophia mumbled, as the others remained silent. The tone of her voice seemed to change. She sounded almost frustrated, and unconcerned with Seth's affairs or lack of presence.

"Well, we can't wait for him. I would assume he wouldn't want to wait on anyone else himself. Isn't he always so bold to say money is a luxury we can't afford? Isn't that his quote?"

The others were amazed by her sudden bold words, but I believe no one was more surprised than Ramiel. What would have been more thrilling was for Seth to hear those very words coming from her.

A rush of mutters escaped the surrounding table, whispers, and even laughter among the others.

Ramiel seemed speechless for a second.

"I think we should continue, Eric." She looked over at me, her expression an innocent one and yet determined.

"I'm sure he'll be here soon," uttered Ramiel, glancing over at the door.

"I'm sure he will, but we can't wait on him."

I believe Ramiel was expecting Seth to pop into view at any minute as he continuously looked over at the door.

"Eric, please close the door," Sophia demanded.

The others glanced over at one another and a hush of whispers erupted among them. "And please lock it when you do."

I rose. All eyes fell on me as I moved over to the door at Sophia's request. The silence in the room grew, whispers and snickering erupted slowly from around the table.

"Sophia, what if he comes?" Ramiel asked. He seemed less challenging than before which I found strange. He'd seemed to almost give up at his request to wait for Seth. I wondered why. He was usually the voice in any argument.

"Then, he shouldn't have been late, or giving lectures if he can't follow his own rules."

Ramiel nodded, taking a drink from his mug and fell silent. The others wanted to praise her bravery.

Wrinkling a nose, she was confused as to why she was challenging anything. Had it ever mattered if Seth was late? He could do no wrong and now something had changed. In fact, it seemed to be something going around with everyone in the cathedral. She had never acted this way before.

I walked out of the office to unlatch the doorstopper. As I was doing this, I disappeared from the view of the others. Struggling with the stopper, I kneeled and lifted the latch. Once freed, I began to move the door towards me when almost immediately a hand came crashing down on the doorframe and harshly shoved it back.

I froze spinning around half startled and terrified to find Seth standing behind me, with a hand against the door. He curved his dark brows wickedly, questioning my actions. I hadn't realized just how tall he was until he was towering over me. The smirk on his gorgeous lips surfaced almost in a cruel, twisted laughter.

I stumbled back awkwardly. No one had noticed him, but I was wrong. Everyone was now looking when I reentered the office followed by the prince himself entering after me. I was pale and speechless with Seth guiding it shut behind us both.

Seth stood in front of the room; everyone was silent. He was handsomely dressed in a navy Armani suit and black tie, with a red silk shirt. His slightly black hair came over his widow's peak. Tall and well-built, he was far too mature for his age. His black eyes danced over our faces with a gleaming look in them.

The Armani suit made his face appear pale, made his hair seem even darker. He looked like the devil himself, raised freely from out of the depths of Hell.

"Starting without me, I see?" he merely said, with a wrinkled, full lip.

He glanced over at Ramiel, and his eyes settled on Sophia, who was trying not to look over at him. She bravely gazed up to challenge his eyes, and he flashed her a smile.

"You're late," she voiced bravely, or perhaps foolishly. Her voice sounded shaky in his presence, slowly losing its authority.

"I do apologize, my dearest," he said, she blushed.

The word "mother" seemed to be deleted from his lips with difficulty. Was he upset at Sophia for lecturing him in front of us? It didn't seem like that. He didn't even look mad, just calm and well-mannered. Could Sophia have judged him too cruelly?

"I was simply saying goodbye to Nath—"

"Your *father*," she interrupted him.

"Father," he corrected himself. There was something about that. Seth had always referred to his father on a first name basis, mostly around us or others but avoided such disrespect around Sophia. He seemed to not care this evening, or had forgotten altogether.

"I wanted to say goodbye before he left. He was walking out when I caught up with him. I was able to talk to him for a little while. After all, I promised I would." Seth's smile glowed down at her.

Sophia seemed to blush.

"Yes, you did...promise," she could only say.

I felt sorry for her, feeling Seth was playing an evil and wicked game with her. I knew him a little more than I wanted the pleasure of, and it was an ugly secret I carried with me.

The room was silent. Sophia looked upset and embarrassed.

"I'm sorry I was quick to accuse you of anything less..."

Seth walked around the table where Sophia sat, stood behind her chair, and put his hands on her shoulders. Sophia trembled as she felt his hands, and then his breath against her cheek when he kissed her.

"It's alright, you've gone through quite an ordeal...if anyone should apologize it should be me for not keeping you safe," Seth softly whispered.

"That is one of my duties...as head of this business." He looked around the table meeting our stares, no challengers gazed at his eyes. He turned his attention to the seat beside Sophia. Damien was settled in, and she looked startled when his eyes regarded her intimi-datingly.

A furrow of his eyes, discouraged her hopes and even far more when he signaled her to move aside with a shooing gesture.

I thought she would refuse, but instead she cowered and slipped away to the next vacant seat beside her.

It was well known Damien was the boss of us all, a rowdy and voicing person. It was as well-known as her desires and crush on Seth. Sometimes, she hated him, but at other times, she couldn't say a bad thing about him. When he was near, she seemed to be unable to control her affections for him and she became timid and easily manipulated, like she was in some kind of trance.

"WELL, SHALL WE BEGIN?" Seth asked, from his seat beside Sophia. He leaned back and put his arm around Sophia's chair now settling into his position with more ease.

Sophia looked uncomfortable, unable to sit back. I worried...

11

THE ACCEPTANCE

SETH

The dreams of her had left me intoxicated and far more aware of who I was and who she was to me. It was no longer this reality. This was a fantasy and our reality was beyond. But how could I make her see such? Ramiel talked about being patient that the dream would reveal more. With time, Sophia would come to see the connection between us, but I no longer wanted to wait. I couldn't be forced to live this lie. She had to know this was not who she really was. She must know. Had all her distance looks, been just that? Mere looks? I didn't want to believe it. She knew, but she didn't want to accept it, because the illusion hadn't allowed her to see beyond. It was up to me to make her see the truth, no matter what Ramiel said.

I leaned on Sophia. Her body trembled as my lips inched against her ear.

"Did you dream about me last night?" I asked. I hoped that the dream had awakened something within her. "I...*dreamt* of you," I whispered.

· · ·

SOPHIA GLANCED UP, perplexed, wrinkling her pretty nose quizzically at me. Her eyes were slightly shocked. Her mouth dropped slightly into a gap, but no words would leave her lips.

She, instead, turned away, trying to keep her attention to the table, where the others were vigorously discussing Cathedral events. However, I whispered again. I was intoxicated, having to recall our moments, my desires growing between us. I wanted it to be, I wanted her more than ever. "I dreamt we *fucked*," I whispered gently into her ears. "We made love in a rose garden...do you recall?"

She looked confused, but far more disgusted and shocked by what I had revealed, unable to speak suddenly. There was fear in her eyes and far more confusion.

There was doubt on her face. Her heart was beating wildly. Images of the dream resurfaced in my mind, unable to resist doing so. I was aroused. I wanted her to feel what I felt. I felt her, recalling as I pressed against her. My pecker pushed hard and dry inside her and my lips on her neck breathing hard at every thrust. I couldn't stop; I wanted her.

I reached out, dropped my hand, placed it on her thigh and quickly pushed her dress up, then between her legs. She flinched grabbing at my hand when she realized what I was doing. She darted her eyes around while widening them. Did she want it? Was she *enjoying* it? Would she welcome my touch, my fingers if I moved them up her thigh, caressed and rubbed her sex? Would she resist? Would she breathe heavily and hard at my thrusts with every forceful stroke of my hands? I could make her whimper.

"Stop!" her lips hissed, biting hard at her mouth. She pushed at my hand until I had no choice but to retract from her crotch.

Why was she resisting when in our dream we had been more then touching? Something had a hold of her, *something* evil would not let her see!

She looked uneasy, pulling down at her dress to cover herself. The shame resurfaced upon her face as I had seen in the dream. She blushed, quivering almost in tears. I didn't know what to say, or what to do. I didn't want to hurt her, but she needed to know the truth of us. I wanted to smell her, to taste her as I had before. I felt the nectar of her pussy glazing and slippery upon my fingers.

I leaned over upon her hoping to ease her fears and confusions of me. I was hungry for more. My loins were growing and on fire. I was breathing heavily, like in the dream, and filled with desire and unstoppable hunger.

"I want you to... You need to know the truth...the truth about us. About the way I feel for you."

"Your making no sense," she growled keeping her voice down. "And this behavior..." she took a breath unable to speak further of the whatever confusion that suddenly had a hold of her.

"We need to talk," I hissed biting at my lips.

"What's wrong with you?" she angrily snapped in a whisper, trying to avoid catching anyone else's attention.

She couldn't believe what I was saying. I think it was what I had tried to do that she having a hard time accepting. She didn't understand it. I put my hand on her thigh, she pried it away.

"Don't touch me," she sternly said. It hurt more hearing her saying those words, but seeing the features of her face was more painful.

I REMEMBERED THE DREAM; she was standing on the side of my bed. When I awakened, I smiled up at her. She removed her gown and tossed it on the floor, standing naked and lovely. I immediately sat up, but she climbed on top of me pushing me down and pulling at my boxers as she straddled me. I didn't resist. She pressed her mouth against mine as I pushed insider her, the heat and hardness of my dick pulsating in my every thrust. My body was on fire, and I was now wishing I could do that once more.

I moaned heavily, exhaled a breath and through rampage love thrusts, our movements increased between the two of us. The heat of her body baring over me, with every longing, with ever deep passionate kiss, I wanted more. I couldn't satisfy the thirst. I moaned once more; she was a whore in bed. I squeezed her tighter to me aching and longing at the ravaging pounding of her body as it came hard on the top of my penis.

She knew the dream, the same one I had repeatedly.

And now she denied them to me, to herself. Why?

"How could you say that after?" I began to say.

"After nothing. Nothing happened," she quickly said in a whisper, turning her eyes toward the table. Eric was still passing out his foolish paperwork.

"Are you sure? Even you have doubts," I voiced, nearly raising my tone.

"There are no doubts." She bit hard on her lips. Confusion fashioned the creases of her lovely brow. I pulled away and grabbed at my penis. As hard as it was, I knew not what to do with myself having envisioned the dream once more in my head.

Sophia looked anxious to leave, or escape was the better word. I couldn't leave it like this. What would Ramiel say? He was already looking over at me curiously and concerned. He would lecture me, although this was all his fault.

I dropped back upon my chair exhausted and aching for her affections. I settled for resting my arm upon the top of her chair, adjusted on the seat, so that I was facing Sophia, with my back to Damien. A better view, a better way to hide what I wanted her to see, the hardness and the need to be inside her. I tried to look ahead, to distract myself from the aching of my groin as the meeting continued.

I caught her glancing over as I adjusted the massive boner beneath the navy slacks. Her head spun back, and she bit her lips stirring in her chair. With that glance, I knew she had dreamt of our encounter together, of our moments in bed, of our heavy sexual adventure in the meadow of roses filled with deadly thorns ripping at her dress. I loved that dream; it was my favorite. Watching from a distance as she walked toward me, as the thorns ripped at her gown until finally, she came to stand before me, and the pieces left began to fall freely around her leaving her naked. I couldn't help myself as she guided me to the ground, and I pushed my dick inside. Like the first taste of a dessert touching my palette.

If this continued, she could not imagine what she would have to do to end it all.

12

THE WICKED

ERIC

I logged the time of the meeting, unable to keep my eyes away from Sophia and Seth at the other end of the table. Seth leaned over Sophia's shoulder, whispering into her ear. I could only guess what he could be telling her. But the expression on her face troubled me, and I wanted to come in between whatever was being said. Among all the chaos, the others were taking their turns expressing their concerns to Ramiel, while the handsome white-haired owner addressed each of their problems with no interest. He looked rather bored, as always.

We usually started our meeting in this manner. At the other end of the table, Santiago seemed to be the only one completely bored with the whole display.

Damon, who was six-feet tall with long black hair, was next in line. The thirty-year-old vampire was in basic black, like the rest of us. He wore leather pants most of the time, and a leather vest sometimes. He painted his face white, his nails black, stained his lips slightly red, and like the rest of us, wore fangs. Silver rings as well as necklaces hung from around his neck, and a Satanic pentagram with his name carved on the metal cleverly stuck out from the rest. He had made it himself, and seven others just like it for the vamps, with their names on them, including Sophia's and Nathan's.

Damon, a kindly and calmer vampire, but religious at heart like his companion Damien, who was slightly older than him, was today wearing his black slacks instead of his usual vest and trousers. A long trench coat Sophia had given him for his birthday hung from his thin frame. He smiled, showing off his canines, pinning his tongue between his teeth, when the others gave him their undivided attention, and Ramiel glanced over at him.

"I think that sometimes...*maybe* there should be something else served on the dinner plate every Wednesday. Instead of the same *chicken*...I guess what I mean is the chef could get *creative*, I suppose." Damon finished up by looking down at the table. He was always the shy type, and never was known to be so outspoken. Although a tall guy, he had a kind heart and sweet nature.

"Creative, Damon?" I repeated, trying not to be rude, hoping Seth would not bite his head off for making such a silly suggestion. However, it seemed Seth was too busy talking to Sophia. He hadn't been listening to anyone, nor had he said anything since he had come into the meeting. Sophia had preoccupied him the whole entire time. That didn't surprise me, though it worried me.

Damon unexpectedly spun around, his innocent eyes staring right at me like a child caught with his hand in the cookie jar. I instructed him politely to finish, hoping not to get the attention of Seth, or to bore Ramiel with such a silly concern. But it seemed Ramiel was already bored; he tried to appear interested, though.

"Okay, I'm finished, sorry," Damon softly mumbled, and dropped into his chair with his arms crossed.

"I'll see what we can do, Damon," I said.

Ramiel glared over, folding his lip back. "I see," he said. "Is that it?" he asked, curving his lips in a gentle grin. The tone of his voice was stern and arrogant.

"Perhaps we can monitor the chef, or place requests ahead of time, and make choices about what is wanted instead of the having the same everyday thing," I suggested to Ramiel, who turned slightly to me. His face read, seriously?

I caught him turning toward Seth. I wasn't sure if he was trying to get his opinion or a suggestion, but when he realized he had to deal with this, he took a breath.

"Is this honestly a problem?"

Damon stirred in his seat. I didn't know what to say to this. It was obvious he thought it was a stupid request. He was usually outspoken, but for whatever reason he held back. I wondered if it was because of Sophia. It seemed he was trying to observe what was happening with them from beside him.

"I can speak with the chef; that won't be a problem, Ramiel?" I offered to ease the tension. He exhaled loudly, like he was bored with the whole display.

"Do as you will," he said, shooing me with a movement of his hand.

"Sure, I'm on it, Ramiel," I said, tucking back a lip, and biting it. The others shot me glances of concern and uneasiness.

Of course, all this would mean filling out forms to do so.

"Thanks!" Damon said from across the room as I wrote on my note pad.

I rose to begin distributing the stack of papers Sophia had given me when Seth tossed a folder over to me. It was a personal one he had brought along with him.

I froze, looking back at him with uneasiness and dread. Ramiel didn't say a word; he was leaning back with the same display of boredom and taking another drink of his coffee mug.

Sophia's had dropped her head down, unable to meet my eyes. She looked troubled, and so seriously lost in thought that not even she said anything about Seth tossing me the folder.

"Distribute that," Seth said, with a smirk. "And get me a cup of coffee while you're up. You know how I take it." He grinned broadly again, this time at the empty air.

Yeah, I knew. I ground my teeth. "Asshole," I whispered under my breath.

The room turned incredibly silent as I moved to the back. I heard Ramiel, Seth, and even Sophia talking momentarily as I walked over to Seth's desk, where the coffeepot was set up. I took a large black mug from the table, one with the words "The Sarvakkian Prince" in red imprinted on it and poured hot coffee into it. Then, I turned and glanced back.

At the other end of the room, Angelo rose; it was his turn to address the table and Ramiel with his concerns. I heard his voice and turned my head slightly back to see. Seth's and Ramiel's eyes were both on the white ghost Angelo, and although anyone would have been terrified, he seemed undisturbed.

Ramiel put his cup down and listened with the same uninterested look as before. Seth was impatiently tapping his fingers on the table, while examining the vamps with a crude smile on his face.

The others were avoiding his eyes, either by looking down or at each other. The room was so quiet when Angelo took the floor, you could cut the tension with a knife.

Seth sternly looked over at me, just as I put the spoon down and picked up the cup.

"I'm *waiting*," he impatiently hissed; then, he slightly leaned against Sophia.

No one came to my aid. Not Ramiel, nor Sophia, who was still looking away from Seth's view. At the other end of the table, Angelo began to speak, carefully choosing his words. The others were softly talking to each other and holding private conversations with one another as I walked around the table, with the cup of coffee held firmly in my hand.

"My idea is that perhaps we should get more local bands to play here on weeknights, to hype the place a little bit. That sort of thing goes well with the youth. Something they like, something gothic, most definitely. We can even have celebrity bands! You meet people all the time, boss. How about it?" I heard Angelo say his rather inept speech as I stopped behind Seth's chair.

Seth hadn't even noticed me. I was about to hand him the cup, and then froze as I saw him slip his hand into Sophia's lap. She shoved it away, as she snapped angrily at him. He shot back with his own words, but they were pleas. He wanted to talk to her. I couldn't hear what he was saying, the rest were whispers.

Sophia gasped, as her eyes then found me standing watch behind them. She didn't seem to realize what was happening. Was she under some kind of spell?

Seth suddenly turned and caught sight of me. He didn't seem concerned with being caught. Instead, he frowned at me, far more bothered by seeing me with a curve of his lip he extended his hand to take the cup.

I placed the cup in his hand, and he placed it on the table. I hurried to leave, but he grabbed my arm suddenly. I panicked and tried to pull away first, but he jerked me back harshly. Everyone, except Ramiel, froze in rank and utmost terror.

I tried to remain calm, not to look frightened, but it was hard as he pulled and twisted the skin of my forearm. I held the pain back, biting my tongue as a burning sensation coursed through my forearm.

Seth pulled me close. The same ghastly smile flashed on his face, and his eyes widened wickedly over at me. Ramiel ignored the display. He seemed almost to laugh in a light chuckle.

"Eavesdropping, are we?"

"No, sir," I ground through my teeth. "Just bringing you your coffee."

He glanced at his cup on the table. "Well, you didn't give me the chance to say thank you."

It was what he didn't say that scared me. The anger deep in his eyes, the rage, and the spite.

I shuddered and moved away as he released me. I walked back around the table and picked up the folder, opening it without argument. I tried not to think of what had just happened. The others were quiet; no one challenged him, including Sophia, who seemed to be in her own troubles. I couldn't make sense of any of it. I feared for Sophia.

I glanced over the documents in Seth's folder. Inside, a pile of expenses greeted me from the first page, along with cutbacks and other things that I knew would be focused upon by us. I looked up. Seth was still staring at me, except there wasn't a smile on his face now, just a cruel dry stare.

I began to distribute the stack of papers among those at the table. Slight mumbles and small remarks escaped the lips of the vamps as they got a hold of the papers and noticed what I had feared. The first paper listed the expenses, as well as overall earnings the club had made. The second paper outlined replacements, and any needed repairs. The third recited every cutback of which you could think. Personal requests were on the top of the list. Many of the vamps had figured their requests would be met since Ramiel was here, but now it seemed impossible, and it all seemed to be a waste of time.

Angelo sighed, dropping to his seat, staring at the papers in front of him.

Seth sat up; he placed the papers in front of him as he took a sip of his coffee. Ramiel seemed to come alive at the same time. Sophia made a fruitless effort to look up; trapped between Ramiel and Seth, she looked helpless.

Her poor smile seemed to cry out for my help, but there was nothing I could do. I took a seat on the opposite side of the table, turned at attention towards my bosses.

"In address to Angelo's request for local bands...Ramiel, may I take this?" Seth asked with a smirk.

"Be my guest." Ramiel said, examining his cup.

"Thank you." He took a breath and began. "In regard to your statement to celebrity bands, I have already taken the liberty of seriously considering this issue. I was asked by several celebrity bands to allow them to perform in our cathedral. I've *always* had an interest in establishing a contract with a few of them. The local bands we allow to play here from time to time have strengthened that interest. That is why I have assembled a few celebrity bands to play in future events already schedule for the coming up months." He took a breath as those around the table seemed excited at the news of celebrities performing at our Cathedral. That was great news, I thought. But I should have known there was going to be a 'but' to follow.

"Unfortunately, I'm dismissing the idea for the continuing performance of our local bands, unless they want to perform for free; other than that, we will no longer have them play here. Unless they begin to show some definite promise, and only then we will establish a contract with them."

He took a breath, narrowing his eyes at every single one of us. Our eyes met and he waited as if he thought I would object. When I didn't say anything, he grinned in satisfaction.

"Now, are there any questions?" Seth asked, glancing around the room.

He had everything worked out. He was the chief businessman of the Cathedral, and he never missed a single profitable deal. He had given himself credit for everything. Angelo had lost his chance to impress him or Ramiel, but he had failed to realize that no one could impress Seth.

"Good, then. Now that is out of the way, let's get down to the most important part of this meeting and my reasons for being here. There is an important item I want to discuss with all of you," his voice rose slightly over the silence in the room. It was no longer soft, but was growing more demanding and aggressive. He rose and began to walk the room, coming around the table and each one of our chairs. It was somewhat creepy and uncomfortable when he stopped suddenly at one's chair. The vamps felt a certain uneasiness when he did and froze on the spot, unsure of how to react.

"As you are aware, last night an intruder attacked my mother. This greatly concerns me, not only for her well-being, but it also brings to question the security of our beloved Cathedral. Because of this incident, I was forced to dismiss several members of our security staff for their lack of performance. Now, I hope that all of you are aware it is the responsibility of each one of you to make sure this place remains safe for all, but especially for Sophia, my mother."

Sophia looked up; she seemed to awaken from her trance at the mention of her name. He made it completely around the table coming around to where Sophia was seated stopping at his chair where he had started.

"If that fails, I might be forced to dismiss some of you. And I don't want to have to do that." Seth chuckled at those last words.

There were murmurs of disbelief from the vamps around the table. Sophia seemed to want to speak, but instead lowered her head. Even Ramiel nodded. When the others glanced in his direction for aid, he looked away, agreeing with Seth. His actions didn't surprise me in the least. He seemed withdrawn, and as cold and uncaring as a stone wall.

"It's truly fortunate I was there, and fought the intruder away, rescuing Sophia," Seth continued, this time taking his seat and putting his arm around Sophia. He sounded so cocky. She fell silently against him, trying desperately to return the embrace, but she couldn't.

Seth kissed her forehead as she gazed up at him, almost intoxicated. He smiled wickedly, holding onto her, making no attempt himself to release her.

"I'm afraid her attacker's still out there, somewhere. He didn't fall from the window, as I had thought. Nevertheless, the proper officials have been notified. And for Sophia's safety, I've taken it upon myself to repair the damage done to the window. That way she will be close by me, and I can keep an eye on her."

Ramiel nodded, "I agree."

Sophia sat up slowly; escaping Seth's tight grasp. She seemed dazed, yet fighting to clear her head. "I think I should stay downstairs with the others," she managed in reply. "It's the way Nathan wanted things to be."

"No, Sophia, I disagree," Ramiel protested. "It's best this way. Stay upstairs where Seth can watch over you."

"Yes, Mother, it's best that way," Seth softly hissed.

"You're *my* responsibility when Father isn't here. I *must* insist on this."

She glanced over at Seth, gagging in slow motion. Ramiel and Seth huddled over her in an embrace, like two vultures trying to devour her with their nurturing concerns.

"I think it should be Sophia's decision," I interjected, feeling the need and pressured by the others to speak for her. I found myself doubting there had ever been an intruder in Sophia's room in the first place. I'm not sure why I felt that way. Or perhaps I did, glaring from across the table towards Seth and Ramiel.

Seth darted his eyes over at me so viciously that I wanted to take back my words. His expression said, *this is none of your business.* But it seemed my words had given Sophia a will to fight.

"I will return to my room when Nathan comes back," she boldly and haughtily announced. "Until then, I'll stay downstairs, with the others."

She gazed bravely over at Seth. His eyes were drawn to hers for a long moment.

Then, he suddenly smiled and seemed to abandon the topic. "As you wish ...Mother." The words seemed forced from his lips.

Sophia fell back against her chair, exhausted and unable to escape Seth, who leaned against her and pressed his lips on her cheek. He was, however, aware of my eyes boring holes into him. He looked directly at me and curved his lips in an almost feral snarl.

"Very well now, let us continue." Seth harrumphed as he rose again from his seat and strolled the room coming around to my side of the table

"I've heard only some of your requests," he continued, while walking to the end of the table.

Angelo and Damon raised their hands before he could finish. Seth gazed at them, and then ignoring them, continued.

"Unfortunately, I'm not granting any favors. There will be no exceptions. You don't like the dish of the day? Make or purchase your own. You're not satisfied with the game room or your bedchambers? That's too bad. Just leave. You are always free to go."

Angelo and Damon slowly lowered their hands, feeling like fools. There were whispers from among those around the table.

"Look, no one's forcing you to stay. My rules are simple, and the rewards are plentiful, but not free. Look at the documents carefully. Study them and remember them. These papers are for your information only. Although all the documents are important, it's the third page that should concern all of you. On that page you will find your requests have been cut. As well as allowances, and expansion of the underground vaults. There will be *none*."

The vamp's voices rose slightly; confusion spread throughout the room.

Ramiel and Sophia seemed to be mobbed with questions. Ramiel raised his hand in attempt to stop the vamps from directing their concerns to him. He lowered his voice, pointing to Seth at the end of the table, who was standing impatiently with his arms crossed.

At once, Seth slammed his fist on the table, and startled all of us. The room once again fell silent and still. Sophia looked up, swallowing her shame, fighting an inner demon inside her and trying to avoid my eyes. But when she failed to look away, she smiled innocently at me.

I felt such great, overpowering anger that I wanted to hurt Seth and hold Sophia. Protect her from him in any way. What was happening between them? What had I walked into during that moment I had stepped up? What I had I missed?

Yet everything seemed so clear. No matter how I wanted to deny it and avoid the signs. I understood why he had the pile of pictures of Sophia in his top drawer all along... Why he bought her those short and tight dresses... why he had bought the same fragrance his father wore. Sophia loved the perfume. And it was then that I *knew*.

It had always made sense. Why had he had taken her favorite

perfume bottle? Had I forgotten or doubted what I had seen? Did I want to deny watching him sniffing Sophia's panties, and then tucking them into his pocket? Why had I dismissed this horrible incident?

"*Silence!* You will direct your concerns to me, and *only* me!" Seth shouted over my thoughts. I blinked up suddenly to catch the fire in his eyes.

The scent of Ralph Lauren Romance cologne emanated from his body as he pushed back his long, black bangs. The hair fell back into place over his head. He dressed in expensive stuff: suits, shoes, cologne, anything designer. Though he wasn't obsessed with his appearance, he was obsessed with Sophia.

Seth tossed the papers on the table; his eyes scanned the painted faces. He flashed them a smile, a grim and fearsome grimace. Then, it all came back seeing the rage pouring from his eyes and his expression.

———

HE SLAMMED me against the wall. His smile had refreshed the whole incident in my head suddenly. I felt his breathing had touched my painted face as he began to scream. I thought he was going to kill me, the way he was talking. His large black eyes, and his lips spread wide into a voracious death grin.

He took Sophia's panties from his pocket and placed the fabric over my nose. Her scent collapsed my senses. The mixture of her perfume and the smooth fluids of her body spread over the lining of fabric, erupting from the red garments, and it intoxicated me. I fell on the wall, pressed by Seth's huge form into place, the organ between my legs hardening at the simple swath of cloth he was holding in his hand.

I struggled, fighting my desires and the guilt building inside me. Ashamed that I had enjoyed it, which only made it worse that Seth knew it.

"I didn't do anything. I was only...she asked me to come...I was help—" I stuttered. But he knew.

"Don't deny it. Don't deny what you plan to do to my mother. You were planning on *fucking raping her*? You make me sick."

He carelessly placed the garment back in his pocket.

"Who do you think she will believe, you or her loving son? Especially with the proof I'll provide her?" He chuckled and released me. I slipped to the ground in front of him and began to sob. Then, I heard his voice speak to me again.

"Now I want you to do something for me. A simple act, of an unholy importance."

———

WITH A WRINKLE ON MY NOSE, I jumped yards at the sound of his voice.

"Now, I've noticed a few of you have allowed yourselves to be photographed," Seth went on to say. His gazed dropped over at Santiago and Valentino. The two vamps lowered their eyes, unable to meet Seth's incapacitating frown. "From this point on, there will be a charge for any photographs or autographs, no excuses. Is that understood?"

The vamps nodded, without hesitation.

"Now, if there's nothing else, this meeting is over."

Immediately, the vamps jumped from their seats, exiting the room. I tried to remind them to meet for dinner downstairs, but they disappeared so fast I didn't have a chance.

Seth gathered his paperwork at the end of the table, putting a few items into his briefcase. I rose as Ramiel dismissed himself from Sophia, then shook Seth's hand and disappeared down the grand staircase behind the others. I wondered where he was headed, if he was on his way out and if we would see him again this evening or the following day?

Sophia rose from her seat slowly, like a wounded calf. She trembled making her way carefully around the table. She was making an attempt for the door, eyeing me as if to say, *help me.* I rushed to my feet, but was blocked by Seth's towering form.

"Do me a favor, be a good lad, and take this to my bedroom," he hissed, placing the brief case and stack of folders in my hands. I wondered why when his desk was at the far end of the office. Yet he wanted me to take these items to his bedroom. Surely an attempt to get me out of the room. I thought this would give Sophia a chance to escape, but she hesitated, and it soon became the worst mistake of her life. She stepped behind Seth, unable to move.

"Wouldn't you rather like them on your desk." I insisted. He gave me glare. The vision of him pushing me against the bedroom wall of Sophia's room came into my mind again.

"What part of take these to my room did you not understand?" he rudely said again. I nodded and took the items.

I exchanged glances with Sophia as I walked out the door and up the stairs leading into the corridor of the second floor.

13

SINS OF A SON

SETH

As soon as Eric was gone, she hurried towards the door around me. She looked panicked trying to hurry out.

I came to block her attempts to flee. She shoved back separating herself from me. Moving away into the room by my desk, I slowly shut the door, locking it.

I stepped over slowly.

"Why are you afraid of me?"

"I'm afraid of what's going on with you. What's gotten into you?" she yelled.

"The truth," I said foolishly, stepping up to her. She seemed timid in my presence, in fear.

"The truth? The truth about what?"

"About us, Sophia."

Her face denied it. "There is no us, Seth. I'm confused; I don't understand where all this is coming from? I need to go..."

She moved passed me. I put a hand on her arm and stopped her. She glared back at me pulling at her arm so I would release her, but I didn't.

"Let go."

"You had the dream. You can't deny it. You had the dream and you enjoyed it."

She pulled at her arm. Her lip tightened as she bit down on it. I knew she had done everything I'd accused.

"You can't deny something is happening here, something is happening between us."

"You're mad," she firmly said, walking away.

I rushed over at her and stopped her pushing against her and forcing her upon the wall of the office.

"Listen to me. Tell me you don't believe it. Tell me you didn't dream those dreams." But it was in her eyes, the truth. She had the dreams just as I had. She saw the visions.

"They're only dreams," she sadly announced. "Somehow, I had some influence on you in some strange and ugly way. Forgive me; now, let me go!"

"This isn't your fault," I said. "This is destiny. This is you and I, our real life. This- all around us- this is the fantasy. You're not my mother and I'm not your son, that is the truth. I love you. And you, you must remember you love me."

She screamed, "Stop!"

I neared to kiss her, but she turned her head away. I forced her lips to my mouth, lifting at her dress. She fought me as I dropped to my knees before her and begged her not to turn me away, pushing my hand up her dress.

"Why don't you believe me?" I begged her.

I grabbed at her panties, pulling them down. She fought me with feeble struggles. I immediately reached up and placed my face between her legs. Her breathing became heavy and her struggles seemed to die for a mere moment, it gave way to my further attempts and I began to kiss her coffee-brown triangle. Her breath increased, as I drove my tongue inside her, slipping it deep into her pussy. Sophia gasped, and collapsed to the floor. My tongue continued its descent inside her as she moaned, crying out in organismic delight. Licking at her leg, I rose over her lurching upon her forcefully.

"I love you! I always have...you and I we were meant to be together. We are lost in this world, but we have found each other. I need you. Please, remember us just as I have. It's not your fault you've forgotten, but don't let it separate us any longer. Why do you think you never change? Think about it!" I whispered softly into her ear, squeezing her breasts so hard I came close to pushing inside her, but she groped away from me fleeing to the door. I rose immediately. and raced after her catching her by the entrance before she could escape me. I turned her to me.

"Sophia, please... I love you."

She kneed me hard in the groin. I collapsed groaning in pain as she managed to unlock the door and escape.

For a few seconds I remained staring at the wood of the floor, bearing the pain. I heard her steps fleeing down the long staircase, down into the vaults where she had been staying with the vamp freaks. After a moment, I rose taking a breath and calmly adjusted the tie, then wiped her nectar from my lips. It aroused me further.

I SLAMMED my fist against the wall. Wandering into the empty hallway, I caught sight of the door of the vault swinging shut. I stared into the corridor with longing, but resisted following her. Instead, I descended the stairs, glancing over at the vaults. She was still under the illusion of this world, it's prisoner. Until she was free, she wouldn't believe or accept me. But the desires to go after her were there, thinking about what Ramiel had told me.

I walked across the antechamber. One of the bouncers greeted me halfway down. I ordered the big man to hand me my coat. The large man obeyed immediately, handing me a long, black trench coat. It had been raining outside, and the freezing weather had caught Houston by surprise overnight. Though it was quite cold, the freezing weather only lingered for a week at the most.

I threw the coat over my built figure and dressed for the weather, taking the leather gloves from inside the trench's pockets and putting them on. I ordered the big man to bring the car around. The clumsy fellow ordered another bouncer to bring the Lincoln, tossing him the keys, and then followed me out the door and down the Cathedral steps.

They stopped at the bottom of the steps as the shiny, black Lincoln came around the side of the parking lot. The air was blowing against my pale face, strewing the long bangs of my hair over my fore-head. The cold weather made my cheeks rosy. It never bothered me much. I enjoyed it far more than the hot weather Texas had to offer. I stood at the bottom of the cathedral steps waiting as the Lincoln came to stop in front of me.

The driver got out of the car and walked around it, towards Ralph, who was already standing beside me, shivering uncontrol-lably. I caught the driver nudging the security director as he opened the door of the car for me. I slipped in, then stopped, resting my hands on the door halfway out of the car. I glanced back at the two men, who froze suddenly at my gaze.

"Head down Westheimer; then go to Richmond after that," I ordered, disappearing into the car without another word.

Ralph closed the door, giving the other employee a harmless glance, then a wrinkled smile. I assume they knew exactly where I was headed. It wasn't a surprise to any of them; I frequented those places. Made them keep it a secret, and though I went there a lot, I never stayed long. Sure, I always left in a rush, and afterwards was angry for some reason. Or so they assumed.

Ralph climbed into the Lincoln's driver's seat and buckled his seat belt. He put the car in drive and sped away, with me silently seated in the back of the vehicle.

14

THE RETURN

The true test of anyone's worth as a living creature is how much he can utilize what he has.

The place was crowded with empty take-out cartons of food. Pizza boxes filled with half-eaten crusts lay on the coffee table and on top of the couch. The joint looked like a tornado had recently stormed through it; only certain familiar, homely pieces of furniture indicated that it had been a residence at one time or another, under better circumstances.

Lucas slowly crawled from underneath the empty containers, where he had overturned a couch, using it as a blanket the night before. He propped the couch up slightly, so it resembled an open coffin, then crawled from underneath, yanking his hand back at the slightest touch of sunlight. He shrieked; but once conquering his fear, he seemed to leap from underneath, avoiding the sun flowing from the windows of his living room. He stumbled to his feet, racing in the blinding sunlight to close the curtains; succeeding, he finally collapsed on the side of the wall.

He hadn't shaven in two days, nor showered, nor could he remember the last time he had eaten. But he wasn't at all hungry and hadn't thought much about eating until he glanced about his house and noticed the boxes scattered on the floor.

The taste of blood was still lingering in the back of his throat, and only when he licked his dry lips was he reminded of it. He could even smell it on himself. His new work shirt was covered in blood, and he wasn't sure how it had gotten there. He wanted to lick it, hungrily taste it, but he could only smell it, and he put his face against the shirt, slavering and drooling.

He suddenly stopped as a sound at the other end of the room eagerly drew his attention. A shadow dashed from the corner of his eyes, but when he looked, only a dining chair sat at a distance from him among the thrown furniture.

Again, a sound drove him intensely wild. He listened raptly before looking back across the living room, where the single chair still sat.

A shadow fell over the chair, and at once he began to crawl on his knees towards it. He stopped again and looked away; something had scared it off. No, it was there that he sensed it. He glanced back at the chair, and this time saw it.

Upon the head of the chair, perching like a bird, was a figure with a long cloak. Ghostly white hair draped over its head, and its white, oval eyes brightly sparkled down at Lucas from where it sat. From the folds of its grimace two double canines wickedly smiled down at him, greeting him.

"Please, let me die. Please, I can't take it. I'm so thirsty. So...so thirsty. I need to drink," Lucas softly stated, his voice quavering as he knelt before the form.

It clasped its hands together, still crouched upon the top of the chair in a birdlike perch. It gazed down at Lucas, and there was sympathy in its white eyes for him, but there was also a growing urgency.

"I need you," the pale figure hissed from between blood-stained lips. "And once you've served your purpose, I will grant you anything."

"But it hurts," Lucas mumbled; then he lowered his head and began to weep helplessly.

At once, the form leaped from out of the chair and landed in front of Lucas. It grabbed the terrified young man by his shirt and lifted him off his feet. It took him in its embrace, cutting its own throat with one long, horrible fingernail, and pressed Lucas's lips against the wound.

"Drink, then," the figure said, patting Lucas's head like a mother feeding her thirsty infant.

Lucas tried to refuse, though knowing he longed for it. Knowing he was enslaved by it, he resisted until he could no longer, and then drank eagerly.

The blood rushed into his mouth like a warm reward, filling him with passion, and an intoxicating feeling overcame him. He saw himself running through a tunnel, hands reaching for him from all directions, ghostly faces kissing him through the air. But still he drank hungrily; he didn't understand any of the images.

He saw winged figures flying in purple and red skies, saw a fiery abyss open wide to greet him, and viewed the ruins of an ancient labyrinth. Saw black oceans, planets, and stars, and strange crafts he had never seen before roaming the blackest skies. Saw men in foreign military uniforms he had never seen on earth. Saw worlds he had never seen before, and things he never even knew existed.

In a strange fortress over and past the clouds, a red-haired princess and a tired old man in elegant robes danced in a crowd of rich spectators. When the image changed, he saw himself being nailed to a cross. Saw cowardly peasants scatter, and giant tanks of steel crush and leave lifeless bodies on a burning planet. Saw Roman soldiers marching into war, empires burned to the ground, and others rising. Saw weird metallic creatures, finally saw Death and looked into its eyes, and in their ebony centers he saw Amael's youthful blurry image, dressed in an elegant robe with long, black hair covering his head and shoulders, looking back at him full of wonder. He drank as all the images resolved into one thing alone. Then, he screamed.

15

REALITY

SOPHIA

I awakened and sat up immediately and began to cry. Realizing the reality I was now in. I had awakened from yet another nightmare, sweat draped my brow as I wiped it away. I glanced around the room, feeling a shiver race up my spine. All alone in the large library, I found refuge among the literature surrounding me. The placed looked creepy, but I would rather be here than upstairs or anywhere else.

I looked down at a table; there were a few book piles scattered in front of me. *Sarvakk*, my first novel, lay open invitingly. I picked up the book, feeling over the glossy cover, then opened it, and scanned through its pages.

I read through the Prince's part, the character I'd treasured. Had he been real in some way? Had I put my own memories in the pages of my novel, and not known this? Why did I doubt who I was all of a sudden? Was its Seth's words? And why all the questions?

I reread the part between the Prince and my beloved. An image of myself or another person existing in a past long ago forgotten, or totally abandoned?

What had gone through my mind when I had written this book?

The thoughts, the words had just filled themselves in as if they had already happened. It felt real and right, as though a hand had led me to write it all down.

These characters weren't just creations of me from some deep-rooted imagination. No, they all felt complete, and real! It was as if they had been there, breathing down my neck as I typed every single letter down, talking to me from somewhere deep inside, whispering about each passage, each incident and event that had taken place in their lives.

I loved the character of the Prince. I imagined being his love, Sabelle, clinging in his arms, protected by his powerful being forever and always. It brought a smile to my face, rereading the character's words to Sabelle. His devotion, his love, and finally his death, all for her! It was like Nathan and I, devoted in a love, but separated by duties. It shouldn't have been that way.

A long sadness I couldn't explain enveloped me; something was missing. I hated that Seth's words rang with a sense of truth. There were feelings I couldn't explain, dreams that I could understand. And the idea that he had these same dreams and feelings made me question my identity. I thought of talking to Ramiel. I knew very little of my past, only of what he had revealed, which wasn't much. He had adopted me and brought me here, raised me as a child, then brought Nathan here in the same manner. It was strange how I couldn't remember quite a lot of those days. The only thing he claimed he had not anticipated was us to fall in love. It made me question whether he wanted it to be. He never came between it, but now I questioned his behavior.

However, the uneasiness and confrontation with Seth made me question everything. I held the book in my arms and closed my eyes. I wished the characters were real, I wished my Prince was real. I prayed for him to take me from all this confusion. Nathan consumed my mind now; I hoped he would return soon, like he had promised.

16

PLAYTIME

SETH

Define Good and Evil...

The girls arrived at the hotel room just as I requested. They were the prettiest girls the place had to offer. They always told me that. I was their best customer. They usually gave me a blowjob, then left; I never had sex with them. But for some reason this time it seemed different. I knew it right away when I opened the door and saw them standing in front of me. One of the girls was a blonde, and the other a beautiful brunette with long hair, like Sophia. In fact, she resembled Sophia so much I felt myself harden immediately. I wanted to send the other one away, but decided to add a little spice to the foreplay.

The girls entered the room, but I didn't wait. I grabbed the brunette and began kissing her madly. I groaned, carrying her to the bed as the blonde followed, getting undressed.

No sooner had they entered the bedroom than I was on top of her. I was surprised and excited how much she resembled Sophia; it excited me as I watched her move beneath me. The blonde came to the side of the bed, but I pushed her aside; but hungrily went at her friend, instead.

"Your name is...Sophia," I breathed down at the brunette.

"Whatever you like, baby!" the brunette obediently agreed.

I removed my white silk shirt and hungrily pinned her down, kissing her neck. The brunette wiggled with pleasure as I rolled my tongue down her neck, covering her in kisses.

"What's my name, sugar?" the blonde asked, eagerly trying to get my attention.

I smiled back at the blonde, who sat by the side of the bed. She returned the smile, edging closer. Her firm breasts were revealed through the low-cut tight blouse she wore. She slowly pulled up her skirt and exposed her pale thighs to me. She wasn't wearing any panties, and she began to rub her sex as I looked on. Of course, I wasn't really impressed.

"You just sit and watch. I don't have any use for you," I rudely snapped at her.

She frowned, but obeyed and took a seat a distance from the bed, pouring herself a glass of champagne on the table next to her chair.

I undressed the brunette, slowly touching and feeling her fair skin. She moaned as I came down over her, kissing her breast softly. The girl returned my kisses, helping me unzip my pants. I suddenly stopped her hand and pulled away frustrated.

"No, that's not right. Resist me," I angrily demanded.

The girl seemed confused. I stood at the side of the bed, holding my head in my hands, hoping not to lose my hardon. I pushed back my hair in frustration and ordered her to her feet. The brunette obeyed, standing in front of me in her underwear.

"We're gonna do this...again."

She naively nodded.

"Slowly undress in front of me," I ordered.

I stepped back to watch, taking my pants off and tossed them to the blonde, who with a subtle frown caught them, and set them aside. I pulled my briefs down, and then tossed them aside as well. I stood, naked watching the brunette slowly remove her red lace bra. At least she had worn the right color bra, I thought. I loved the color red. I was growing hard again, and the smile on my face spread as she pulled down her lace panties.

"Good. Very good," I lustfully hissed.

She smiled at me, touching herself as she did so.

"Don't look at me, just do it," I ordered, rubbing my hard dick.

I groaned whispering Sophia's name. I licked my lips all along, watching her with growing anticipation.

"Yes! Very good!"

The blonde rose and wandered over to where I stood. She boldly caressed my bare chest, and erect pecker.

"Let me do that for you, hunk. I'm very good at this."

I grabbed her hand and angrily twisted it, then moved it away.

"Wait your turn! I'm not ready for you, yet."

She painfully squirmed and pulled away from me, stumbling back to her seat where she poured another glass of champagne, and gulped it.

The brunette dropped her lace panties on the bed.

"Turn around and let me get a good look at you," I anxiously ordered.

She obeyed, hungrily looking back at my erect cock.

"I said, don't look at me!" I snapped, stroking myself.

Her eyes immediately dropped to the floor, and she almost seemed bashful. She was innocent and helpless like Sophia. She was anything but, I thought.

"Yes. Now, turn away from me. When I come to you, resist me."

She obeyed and turned her back to me. I slowly walked from behind and immediately grabbed her waist. The strain of myself pushed against her buttocks. I moved my hands over her breasts, excitement raced throughout me.

She nervously shook in my arms, which greatly pleased me. I had her face me, grabbing her face as she did. She fought and resisted me as I kissed her.

"Yes," I hissed, devouring her lips slowly, "Resist...Sophia! Resist." I pushed her onto the bed, immediately dropped over her, and forced my dick inside her. I wanted to relive the moment; I don't know why. It felt right up until the moment it was over.

The girl's soft whispers overcame my moaning.

"No! Stop...No this can't happen!" She cried again taking me back to the moment in her room. I gasped and exhaled her name in my breath.

"Yes, that's right..."

I couldn't stop myself each gasp Sophia's name left my dry mouth. The pleasure grew madly inside me, crawling at the very being of me until in a sheer cry I knew I would have to have the real one. I cried out in ecstasy.

I rose and ordered her to wear the short red dress I had brought with me. I instructed her to dance with me until we had sex again.

"No, this can't be," she mumbled, as my furtive whisper had ordered her to say each time. She didn't question this strange perversion. I suppose she had seen far worse things in her line of work. She seemed to like it.

The blonde finally joined us. I ordered her to get on her knees and to give me a blowjob. I didn't waste time with her, though I had ample seconds of the brunette. I didn't really want Sophia on her knees, sucking my dirty rod.

The blonde wasn't pleased. But hadn't it been she who said she was good at it?

I lay back on the bed, ordered the brunette to sit on my face, and began drinking the nectar flowing from her ebony-chocolate cunt.

I came repeatedly, once again pleasing the illusion of Sophia. She moaned as I held her waist, pressing my lips on the pink flower of her pussy. And when it was all over, I laid beside her as she caressed the locks of my dark hair. I took in a breath, and felt her warm skin alongside me as she stroked my cheek. I never wanted the moment to end. I had only wished it was the real Sophia that lay beside me, not some stupid copy of her.

"What's your name?" I whispered to her.

She boldly replied, "Sophia."

I smiled. "No, your real name?" I asked again.

She seemed to ease and take a breath. I rose to sit on the bed and gazed at her. Her brown eyes found me staring back at her spellbound.

"Laura," she said. "Laura Wat—""

I stopped her. "That's all I need."

She nodded. She seemed possessed by me as she danced in my charm, almost in a hypnotic state. Her face took on a color as I cupped her cheek in my hand leaning to kiss her.

"I'd like to see you again," I said.

She gave me a tiny smile and answered, "Okay."

I PAID the women as they got dressed, slipping an extra two hundred in Laura's panties as I devoured her obedient lips eagerly. She was perfect for the moment.

After they disappeared out the door, I walked over and grabbed a glass of champagne from the table by the bedside. Now, if only I could have the real thing. I drank feeling the sweet nectar run down my throat.

Why did she refuse me, and not believe me? I knew she felt it, just as I had. The connection and the fantasy we were both trapped in. I was the only one that understood the dreams she kept hiding from others. I knew she had them and had been hiding them. When I started having them, they were hard to accept. I thought I had gone mad, that I was some sick fiend. Then, everything became clear. I just wanted the same for her. I needed her, and she needed me. We needed each other.

She must come willingly. Ramiel's words rang in my head, mocking me like an illness. *Willingly?* But she hated me.

The bond was there, strong as it had ever been.

I tossed the glass to the floor, where it shattered into a hundred pieces. I could see it splintering slowly in front of me. Suddenly, an image flashed back from the breaking glass. I fell back; something seemed to knock the wind out of me. I tried to regain my balance and focus clearly on my surroundings.

I felt dazed and confused. The shove came again as the air left my lungs. I gasped as an image once again flashed across my eyes.

A pain raced across my chest. I glanced down at my bare chest, there was a hole ripped into my flesh. I groaned touching the aching wound in disbelief.

My fingers came away with blood. I shook, calling for Sophia, crying out her name and weeping over the roar of my voice. A slow beating began rising quickly. I gazed upward, my eyes covered in tears and fingers drenched in blood. I recognized the beat. Dazed, I realized I couldn't hear my heart, yet the beating increased. In a flash, a figure draped in a black cloak materialized in front of me extending his hand.

I stared down; in the figure's hand was a heart. I groaned, trying to balance myself, and helplessly looked at the form, whose face was now visible.

At first glance, I saw Sophia's face innocently smiling at me. I stumbled back in disbelief, the face changed, and I saw the image of the intruder that had been in Sophia's bedroom.

The figure wickedly grinned at me. His beautiful face bore an uncanny resemblance to my own, enough so that I was overcome with fear.

"I won't let you take her away from me again. Not this time!" the figure shrieked angrily, crushing the beating heart in his hand.

At that moment, I dropped to my knees in horrible pain, clenching at my chest, as the heart he held in his hands was engorged by flames. The echo of the enemy's laughter roared all around me until it finally faded slowly. I collapsed to the floor, the pain slowly easing.

I took a breath and opened my eyes. I could still hear his laughter in my head. It made me quiver slightly. I rose, quickly looking around at this room and at myself. There was no blood, no cuts of any sort on me. I felt foolish for believing a vision that was obviously trying to deceive me in so many ways and to take the one thing I wanted to hold close. It was after her just as it was after me, hoping to separate us, no doubt.

"Mind games." Just foolish mind games, something I'd played on others before. I was still wary, not sure I was alone. Every corner draped in darkness had me cautious and jumping at shadows. After a moment, I eased and poured myself another glass of champagne, staring down at the pieces of glass on the floor.

I recalled the window had shattered in the same manner. I remembered the form falling through it, and over the edge.

Who the hell was this intruder? Why had I forgotten all about him? Would he come back? What did he want with Sophia? And why was he now invading my thoughts? I was afraid for the first time in my life, afraid of losing everything. Afraid of losing Sophia. I feared for my safety. His warning continued to mock me. *I won't let you have her. Not again...*

What did it mean? Ramiel's words rang through of his life before this. He had lived before with Sophia in another form. Was he the one Ramiel had warned me about? Him, as I had referred to him many times before? I refused to give him a name, but did he have one?

"He's more of a demon now. He's in love with Sophia, and he thinks she belongs to him. He won't die. He can't, you see. No, only she can destroy him. Announcing her love to you will stop him." Was what Ramiel had finally revealed? I knew of my past life that I once lived. I had been someone else. Problem was, I couldn't remember whom. That I had lived once before in another plain of that I was sure.

"You expect me to believe that?" I had resisted at first, of course. What sane person wouldn't?

"I don't expect you to do anything," Ramiel firmly answered. "That is the truth. And if you don't come to understand it in time, you will lose everything you've worked so hard for. Including Sophia."

I hardly remembered the rest that had begun the conversation, but before I knew it, I had come to understand and accept my feelings, and realized everything was true. I had gone alone for so long, wrestling with desires I didn't understand. That's when Ramiel had come to me. Those were the first times I felt relieved in having someone to tell my feelings to. I surely couldn't profess them to Sophia, at least not yet, even though I shared everything with her.

"I'm here to help you," Ramiel had kindly said to me one evening as I sat in my room alone, filled with wonder at the thought of Sophia. Never knowing why, I longed to have her, and in the same way that my *fath*—Nathan did.

Her picture clenched tightly in my hand, I studied her fair face, each single strand of her hair magically entwining around my brain as I recalled her from dreams. I tried to imagine her hair as red, as I had once seen her when she wore a red wig at a Halloween party. Why did I like that so much? Or feel a connection to that image of her?

I didn't see Ramiel until the older gentleman had walked a few steps into my bedroom. I was hiding so embarrassed over my feelings. I had to admit I didn't like Ramiel at first. I was jealous of every man close to Sophia.

"Don't you know how to knock? What do you want?" I recalled snapping, quick to hide the picture of Sophia.

Ramiel greeted me with a warm smile, uncaring of by my rudeness, which fueled me more. He walked back to the door. I thought he would leave, but instead he closed the door and wandered back in to stand before me.

"Will you allow me a moment of your time, young Abuda? I need to speak with you."

I ignored him and rose, pushing my way around him. At once, I felt a cold hand at my side; fingers tightly gripped my arm, and pulled at me.

I glanced back in bewilderment and disbelief. Our eyes met. I tried to pull my arm away, but my struggles were pointless. Ramiel seemed to be unmoved by my resistance.

He shoved me, a timid fifteen-year-old me. I dropped onto the small leather sofa I had been sitting on before he had attempted this conversation. His narrow stare now fell right on me. He moved around my room looking at the pictures and collections of a teen boy's room. I had everything one could want. What could I say? We were wealthy, and Sophia sought to please me. Ramiel stopped before me. I was about to protest as his behavior, but when his eyes stared hard at me, I froze for a mere second before I could regain my courage. "How dare you? When my moth— finds out what..."

He wrinkled a side lip at my failed words.

He bent down over me, a condescending wrinkled grimace plastered on his face. I shriveled back, biting down on my lip. I would be the first to admit he frightened me. I tried to regain my bravery, but it was slowly slipping from my fingers.

Ramiel snatched Sophia's picture from my grasp. I didn't try to recover it. My hands trembled slightly. Ramiel examined the picture and began to speak with a smile.

"Now, young Prince. I know how you hate the nickname the vamps have given you, but what you fail to realize is how well it suits you."

"Is that why you've barged into my bedroom, to insult me? Get out. My mother will hear of this, and make you pay dearly for it!" I yelled.

"Your mother is a good friend of mine. I respect her. I would never do anything to harm her, or you."

"Friend? Is that what you call it? You're drooling over her. You're like all the others. You want her, just like every other fool in this world, but you can't have her. All your money can't buy her. Just face it, you're jealous of me, because she loves me."

"Silence!" Ramiel firmly snapped, undisturbed by my insults. The gentle grin reappeared on his face, and it frightened me greatly.

"What do you want?" I bravely rephrased, a little calmer than before.

"To help you."

"To help me? Help me with what? And why should I trust you? I hardly know you."

"Then, we must change that. Don't you think?" he said grinning. He made me turn from him to avoid his smile.

"What the hell are you talking about, old man? What do you think you can help me with?"

Ramiel sat across from me, on the white leather couch. I never really looked at him as I did now. He was dressed in a black jacket, without a tie, and a collarless gray cotton shirt. He had a white nest of shoulder length hair pulled slightly back away from his face. He seemed well put together.

I was bashful, feeling somehow that Ramiel was reading me, plucking my thoughts one by one from my head as well as my feelings, like one does the feathers of a chicken.

Ramiel had a glow about him. His skin was pale like thin paper, and his eyes were a somewhat gray, almost white. I had never noticed before, but two canines sharply stuck out from amongst the rest of his teeth. I wondered why even he had gotten into the fad of wearing fangs like everyone else in the Cathedral.

"I'm talking about your feelings. Your dreams."

I tried hiding my astonishment, but I couldn't stop thinking that perhaps Ramiel had read my thoughts, and the idea scared me. I didn't know what he was capable of, but I suspected a lot more than I was aware of.

"I know what you desire more than anything, Seth. I can help you achieve it."

"I don't know what you're talking about. You know nothing about me." But my voice was very uncertain and shaky.

"I know more than you think. I know why you bite your lips when you say the word "mother," why you cringe at the sound of the word itself."

I flashed him a glance, stirring in my seat. How did he? He couldn't possibly know what I felt or why I resisted this illusion- for that's what it was, a wicked illusion of some evil to keep me away from Sophia, my love. Ramiel placed Sophia's picture on the coffee table in front of us. He seemed to dare me to reach for it the way his eyes darted towards it then back to me.

"You know nothing!" I snarled, rushing to my feet and grabbing the picture from the table. I clenched it tightly against my chest. In embarrassment, I exhaled, turning away from Ramiel, who rose slowly and took a single step towards me. I sobbed silently, laughing in between sobs as I did so, still clenching the picture tightly in my grasp.

"You know nothing."

"Perhaps I don't. Tell me." His expression softened and he seemed more caring. It set me off slightly that his features had now seemed fatherly, drawing me to feel comfort. How was that?

At that moment, I wanted to spill my heart out to him. What if I could share my darkest secret with someone that would understand my pain? I took a breath, feeling my grip on the picture lessen as I looked up at him. He pushed a strand of my hair away. I felt no judgement from those large grey eyes of his, only reassurance and understanding.

"It's hard...so hard to love someone you can't have. To desire her and not have her. Because God Himself said it can't be. Damn them. Damn me..." I bit my lips.

He reached a hand to my cheek. I recoiled, but froze as his fingers wiped at the single tear that had rolled down my face.

"I know."

I glared at him suddenly. Did he honestly? I pulled myself away from him, swallowing the pain as well as further tears that wanted to escape from my eyes.

"No, you don't! No one knows the pain I must face each time I see her. I'm sick. I must be. What else can it be? But it feels right. I must be sick..." There could be no other answer of why I felt such affection for her, that she and I were two people that had been connected by an eternal love. But how could it be when in this life we were far from that?

Ramiel walked over. I felt him near, and slowly turned and hopelessly glanced up at him, clenching the picture against my chest.

"Will you tell my mother? Will you take her away from me? She can't be around me." I was a mess. I saw no other reason. I shouldn't be near her.

"Never. Seth, listen to me; you're not mad or sick. Your feelings are right," he said to me.

I was immediately surprised, far more astonished.

"But how can they be? She will leave me if she knows. She'll stop loving me." I was sure of this. There was something wrong with me.

My grip on the picture tightened as I fought with my emotions. I tried to be brave and strong around Ramiel, but I couldn't. I had lost more than my nerve and weakened before him. Part of me wanted to hear what he had to say. I felt there might be hope, but the other part of me couldn't even face him. I was filled with a dread and embarrassment.

Suddenly, Ramiel embraced me. I surprised myself by not recoiling or flinching away. Instead, I dropped into his arms with a whimper.

"I won't let that happen. I'm here to help you. I will try to explain the dreams and a portion of these things that are happening to you. Your feelings and your strange desires for Sophia, who happens to be your mother in this reality..." I lifted my head and blinked quizzically over at him. *Reality?* "Oh yes." he said, "all this is an illusion; one created to keep you imprisoned in here." He pointed to his head then his heart. "Your feelings are nothing to be alarmed about."

"A portion?" I snapped, pulling away from him, wiping at the tears that had rolled down my cheeks. "Why only a portion? You don't understand, I want her! I want to be with her! Everything about her arouses me! Her smile, her scent! It's like we're meant to be together! And my father...I find myself despising him every day.

Growing restless like an encased animal. I feel he's my enemy, that I should be wary of him. And you say you can only tell me a portion! If there's a reason for my insane behavior I need to know."

"Seth."

I remembered being frustrated and embarrassed at first with the older gentleman for revealing my desires. The frustration and feelings were overwhelming, but the fact that Ramiel had disclosed my bitter secret first had eased my concerns.

"She is not your *mother*, Seth. She's you wife, your lover. And I will make you see that. I will destroy the illusion that has imprisoned the both of you." His hand reached out, pressing his fingers to my temple and a flash of a dream emerged. It was more clear than any dream. I believed it, felt all my senses came alive. I could smell and feel the air against my skin and saw all that he wanted me to know. It was real, everything that I felt. Our life, our true life, a life where me and Sophia were together in love. She was different then. She had a mane as red as blood and was youthful as she was now. An immortal, Ramiel's words echoed in my head. I was dressed in the robes of a prince, with hair as dark as the night and skin as pale as the snow that fell from all around us. There was a palace with large golden peaks and ships that descended into the heavens and beyond.

I gasped as his fingers pulled away, blinking at the visions of beauty he had shown me. "Not visions," he corrected, "but your life. Your true past life. This, what you see now is merely the illusion imprisoning the both of you."

He convinced me, not by mere words, but by showing me everything I'd known and somehow forgotten.

———

I TRIED NOT to think about it. I grabbed the shirt from the chair and my coat, pulled up my pants and straightened my tie, then I walked out of the room, closing the door behind me.

17

THE RELUCTANT VAMPIRE

ERIC

What good are friends if they can't do you any good?

I met with the new bartender earlier in the day. He was on time, and elegantly dressed. I was glad he had a fashion sense of his own. He was quite young, with shoulder length, dyed bright red hair and large round eyes. He was extremely pale and thin, but then most of us did. He was wearing a long cloak, and beneath it was a vest and a pair of black slacks. His lips were slightly discolored; he seemed hungry, as if he was wasting away. There was something else strange about him, too. He looked like he hadn't slept in days, and he seemed slightly paranoid. His neatness in appearance and his quick answers to my questions soon overruled any doubts I had in hiring him.

I walked him through the Cathedral, avoiding Seth any way I could. The Cathedral was crowded, and Angelo was by the bar, busy as always. I brought him over there. The club patrons crowded the stools, greeting us as we passed them by. I smiled back, yet Lucas seemed to be eagerly searching the dance floor. I beckoned him, tapping him on the shoulder. He jumped up as a sigh escaped him, and then walked over to me.

"When will I meet the owner? Don't I have to?" he suddenly asked, with so much expectation growing in his soft voice that it made me wonder why.

"You *don't* want to meet him," Angelo answered as he came from behind us.

He'd been standing at the other end of the bar, wiping the counter. His boyish face was hidden beneath the glittering sparkles of his makeup. He was beautiful, his long hair white with highlights of blue, and his makeup matched the color of his hair. Sparkles of light glimmered from his pale cheeks, and crystals shimmered pasted on the ghostly eyebrows. His eyelids were a frosty blue, with just a hint of black liner, and his lips were a light blue. He wore white and light blue colors. He was the exact opposite of the rest of us.

Lucas spun around just as I did. Angelo introduced himself, dropping the cloth on the bar counter, greeting us with a smile, flashing us a custom pair of double fangs from those bluish sparkling lips.

"So...you must be our new bartender?"

There was a slight hesitation in Lucas; perhaps he was dazzled by Angelo's appearance, as most were. Angelo was the only one of us who wasn't gothic.

No, he had his own style. He mostly resembled a nymphomaniac angel.

Slowly, Lucas extended his hand and shook the bartender's.

"Name's Angelo. Welcome to the Cathedral De Los Vampiros. This is my lair," Angelo smirked, referring to the bar.

Lucas glanced about him, seeing a variety of liquor bottles sitting neatly across the back counter. Wine glasses and beer mugs hung upside down from holding hooks on the frames above the bar.

"So, why *not?*" Lucas suddenly asked. "I mean, why wouldn't I want to meet the owner? I heard she's very pretty and nice. Wait a minute, did you say 'he?'" he stammered, almost instantly forgetting everything else.

Angelo grinned, and the smile on my face spread as well.

"Oh, you mean Sophia. Oh, yes, she's *hot!*" Angelo blurted, and then bit his tongue, catching the frown of disapproval on my face.

"I mean, she's great, and very beautiful."

"Yeah, who did you think I was talking about?" Lucas asked, trying not to laugh as Angelo corrected himself under my instruction. "Who is 'he?'"

Angelo didn't smile; instead, he frowned slightly as a sigh left his lips. Lucas felt uncomfortable, fearing he had misjudged the nice-looking vampire.

But at once, Angelo gazed past him, the frown still spread over his face as he signaled for us to look over at the top of the staircase. Coming down the steps was Seth, right on cue. He was looking wildly around, as if in search of someone.

"Heads up, Eric. I think he's coming this way," Angelo warned me.

"Yeah, I think he's looking for me," I said nervously, trying to hide behind the heads of the patrons.

"Who's he?" Lucas asked, gazing with whetted interest at the tall, pale figure coming down the steps, dressed in a navy suit and red tie.

The man was handsome, he noted, with black short hair, which fell over his eyebrows. Lucas watched him carefully stepping onto the dance floor and be greeted by a security guard at the bottom of the staircase.

Angelo hurried to his work, mixing the drink he already had in his hand, and handed it to a patron across the bar.

"Our mean boss is here. Just sit by, and don't say a word, okay? Take notes, look busy, but don't get his attention. Believe me, you don't want it."

Lucas nervously shook his head, and took the notebook and pen from Angelo's hand to take down anything important.

I made my way around the bar. My eyes still focused on Seth. I followed him through the crowd. He seemed to glance over at the bar, but either he didn't notice us, or didn't care. He kept on walking, moving through the crowd with the security guard and the bouncer escorting him through the dancers.

I looked around for the others; they were all on the dance floor; the Elders were by the door, picking those they felt should enter. Everyone was where he or she was supposed to be.

I looked back at Angelo. He was flipping a liquor bottle in the air, and then catching it, pouring it into a shaker. I called him over. He took the money from a girl customer, blowing her a kiss as she skipped away to the dance floor with her drink.

"Angelo, have you seen Sophie?"

"*Nope.* Hey, did you see *that?* He didn't even come over here."

"Yeah, I know. I'm worried about Sophie, though. I don't want to leave her alone with him."

"Why?" Angelo asked, clearly perplexed.

I knew I didn't have time to explain what I felt and feared. Perhaps it was foolish, or perhaps I thought he wouldn't believe me. I knew Angelo wasn't that type of person. He had been a good friend for a long time, and was the most generous of souls.

"Just a feeling," I muttered.

He didn't ask again; perhaps it made sense when considering Seth was an asshole, and he might say something cruel to his mother to hurt her feelings.

"I haven't seen her since the meeting, and she didn't come down to dinner. She usually joins us."

"I know, that's why I'm worried."

"Don't sweat it. She's probably spending some time with the Prince."

Poor Angelo; even he hadn't realized how scary that sounded.

"That's what I'm afraid of," I muttered.

But Angelo didn't hear me; taking another order, he left me by the side of the bar with Lucas seated closely nearby, rapidly taking his notes.

18

THE DREAM COMES TO REALITY

SOPHIA

You have been cursed. Every day you are the recipient of very real and magically formidable curses.

I gazed across into the empty streets, taking a tiny sip from the wine glass in my grasp. I could feel my head spinning from the alcohol in my veins, but still I drank hoping that any minute Nathan would call. He hadn't, and I began to cry.

Westheimer was beautiful. The streets and the lights sparkled, and people walked along the sidewalk without a care in the world. I could hear the traffic, see people waving as they spotted me under the arched window of the arcade passageway, connecting and leading into the south dome away from the foyer.

The Cathedral was divided with its south and north domes to each side of the building. The passageway guided the visitor into the other connecting buildings, where areas like the library and the theater were located.

The Cathedral was enormous, containing an amazing amount of

craftsman detail and elegantly austere beauty. The descent into these huge domes was breathtaking. A gallery encircled the main dome from the second floor, and to look down revealed the center, where a single chandelier barely touched the marble floor below. Though both domes were made in the same manner, the north dome housed the theater and was the only dome without a chandelier in the center. In its place, a large audience area occupied the dome. In fact, most of the dome was the theater, and not the sitting area. The domes were large, but not as huge as the main dome, where you entered the Cathedral vestibule.

It was under the encased arched window that I sat this evening, on the first floor in the arcade passageway, a step away from the south dome.

I stared out of the large arched window, unframed and opened to the elements of this place. Again, the wind was blowing with that horrifying howling, suffocating the air with a kind of hollow emptiness. My hair was flapping in the fingers of the wind. It felt like the touch of ice on my skin, like frost nibbling at my nose and cheeks, and I began my usual pronounced trembling.

I climbed upon the large window and sat, folding my legs; across from me was a bucket of ice with a bottle of champagne. A small platter of finger foods sat beside it, untouched and sealed with a plastic container.

I took the bottle from the bucket, and poured myself another glass of champagne. Holding it tightly in my hands, I began thinking of Nathan once again. Remembrances of him became perverted with thoughts of Seth forcing me down to the ground. I felt sick, as flashes of the incident devoured my innocent moment. I could feel his breath, his hands on my body. I fell against the wall silently, letting the glass drop from my hand, and then began to cry uncontrollably. What had come over him? Why did I doubt this reality after what he had revealed? The dreams he claimed we shared were, in fact, dreams I had seen myself. Doubts were starting to fill my mind.

Was I *weakening*? Did I believe it? I feared that the moment would come that I would give in. Even when I knew it was wrong, even when I knew I had doubts stirring in me from some deep dark part. There would come a time when I wouldn't be able to stop him, or to fight any longer.

"Oh, my Prince...I pray you really exist. I wish you were here. If only to make sense of this world, which I have so foolishly fallen prey to. Hear me..." I said aloud, in reference to the storybook character.

I bit my lip, only regretting that I had named my son after the character I had grown to love. What a mistake. Was I being punished for that?

I lay against the dry, brick window, tears still pouring from my eyes. I continued crying even after I closed them, as the sounds of the street slowly faded into my listless, completely unreachable dreams.

19

SWEET DREAMS ARE MADE OF THESE...

SOPHIA

From between the trees *it* towered over the forest, and the branches barely touched the walls. The round towers resembled Parisian buildings of circa 1360. The peaks reached into the sky, lost somewhere in the darkness and no longer visible. The eerie but beautiful Palace, not dissimilar in type to Italian fortresses, palaces or town houses, was like the Palazzo Medici, except that it was executed in the late Gothic mode.

Thick vines crawled over the side of the white building; vines filled with thorns which ripped into the marble. The scent of roses filled the air; red living roses blossomed from every direction imaginable.

In a single moment, the entrance of the huge palace slowly opened. The large gates were designed and decorated in holy images, as though they themselves told the tale of the great battle in Heaven between God and the devil. A large image of the virgin holding the child Christ as the ultimate object of all learning was astutely framed by the signs of the zodiac, and the occupations of each demarcated month.

Below the Christ, a large rose separated the next chapter in the web of deception and confusion that followed yet another mark upon the devil, the tale of the Sarlovakk Dynasty.

Inside and beyond the metal gates, a huge garden of roses bloomed, surrounding the path, side-by-side. The garden was designed with large columns, with white lily-shaped formations that left off where they met the curve of each conoid's arch and the ceiling. Half of these lilies were used in series on two sides of a hall space. Transverse arches provided shade for the rose garden, like a fishnet filled with souls and imprisoned in smooth rose petal red walls. The pendant vaults formed a series of conoids all around.

A single narrow path led to a variety of doors. Inside, the doors were all designed in early thirteenth-century detailed stained glass, all showing the signature of the Sarlovakk, *the rose.*

The doors opened to reveal the great corridors of the Palace inside. In the distance, the large rose design was visible. It was both the sun and the rose, a two-pronged symbol of Christ as the new sun and Mary as the "rose without thorns," in the words of the litany of Loreto, taken from the great Chartres Cathedral. The fabulous rose window, from an early thirteenth-century design, *Transept arms clasped magnificent roses!* With careful observation, the symbols had not changed, but the meaning had. The new sun still represented God, or some form of God, but the rose had sharp, deadly thorns.

And the words read, "rose with thorns," *the poison.*

In the center of this magnificent chamber, a central pier fanned open into an umbrella-like vault, where ribs were gathered at the corners of an octagon. Except for a low blind arcade just above the benches of the chapter, the walls were glazed with pointed windows of a moderate height, comfortable and well-lit.

This great chamber was decorated with nave piers widespread; vault ribs took off from brackets shaped into human heads halfway down the triforium band. The slender shafts of the nave and the triforium piers were of dark Purbeck marble. The wall area was decorated with black scrollwork on a red ground, the capitals and moldings were gilded and painted, and only the vault was left white.

A ridge rib should have run all along the center of the vault, with additional ribs for the standard four-part bay. The result should have been a virtual parade of star-shaped designs. But without a ceiling, only an opening, an endless, dark sky (far darker than the one in Hell) was viewed. It was like a whole different world, with aisles and naves, webbed in a life of independent interior arrangement, that of French standards, and English traits.

It stretched into a labyrinth. Beyond the aisle of the cathedral's sculptural marble, another well-detailed, large metal gate guarded its secrets from prying eyes.

The chapel was lightly-lit, and there were other doors around, revealing several different directions. An enormous light grew at the end of one corridor.

The light sparkled blindingly, and then simply withered. Far in the distance sat a throne, built out of thorns and rose vines, with rose heads decorating the sides. These had all withered and dried up with time.

In the center of the chapel stood a figure. I found myself in this place, walking like a drifting zombie. I stepped onward, hearing my own steps beating against the marble floor beneath my bare feet. I felt drawn to the shadowy figure. He was turned away, so I couldn't see his face.

I hurried with urgency to his side, stopping a step away from the form. At once, the figure whirled around, and then suddenly grabbed hold of my arm.

I panicked, pulling away. I gazed up at the stranger's face. As his eyes slowly met my, it sent chills up my spine though they sparkled in a warm smile. His gorgeous face was glowing, with dangling blonde hair falling about his shoulders, glimmering around his face. He was beautiful, glimmering like a great burning light.

I froze, but I wasn't afraid. I didn't know why.

I fell into his arms. He bent forward and pressed his lips against mine in a long-awaited kiss.

"I've found you at last!" The figure whispered, squeezing me
tightly in his arms. "I won't let anything separate us again."

I held him tightly, weeping joylessly as I did.

"Sabelle..." he hissed as he kissed my neck, ardently yet softly.

I felt intoxicated by his touch; weakened. I lay in his embrace,
feeling his lips kiss me sweetly. His gentle touch moved me tenderly.
His rich lips were sweet and alluring, hungrily kissing my own, yet
his desire was pure and innocent.

In a trance, I opened my eyes, realizing that instead of an angelic
face, a withering older face with bitter and fragile lips and eyes so
gray and rage-filled looked upon me. From the wrinkled, sunken, pale
cheeks a wicked grimace unfolded from twin earthen lips as he held
me tightly to him. The long blonde golden strands were gone, and in
their place were long black strands of hair flowing down his shoulders
and over his head, like cobwebs made alive by the tiniest blowing
warm currents of the air...

I screamed.

"This time you won't escape me! You're mine forever!"

At once, I felt pulled back; the frightening figure was racing after
me as I moved away from him. I was gliding, floating from him, faster
and faster until he was a tiny speck on the ground. Another's arm
held me tightly, and I saw we were floating in the sky over the
decaying grounds beyond them.

I looked up and saw but a glimpse of a pale face and white cotton
hair. He had carried me off, white wings spread over his back as he
moved across the sky with me in his arms. The stranger briefly
glanced down at me, but for a second I caught the sight of his familiar
face. And nestled on my lips like feathers was his holy, sacred name...

20

HE COMES...

SETH

"Ramiel?" I called out, entering the passageway. I would have sworn I heard voices, or a voice. The bouncers had left me alone to go to the north dome, and now I wished they had followed.

I walked slowly down the long passageway, glancing out the arched windows as I passed every single one and came closer to the south dome's entrance. From a distance, I saw a shadow—perhaps I hadn't been mistaken about seeing someone in the passageway. But this time, instead of calling out, I hurried silently, hoping to catch whoever had entered the passage.

As I approached, I saw a man dressed in a long black cloak bent over a woman's body. I didn't think much of it. In fact, I thought a couple had come into the passage to get romantically acquainted. I would soon get rid of them, and scold Ralph for letting them get past security. As I got closer, I noticed something odd: the figure was licking the woman's neck, sucking at her throat. As I came closer, I realized the woman was Sophia.

I gasped, almost losing my breath in horror, and rushed over, leaping onto the vampirical figure. I threw the intruder aside, screaming for security at the same time. I pushed the being against the brick walls of the passage, and struggled with him. The monster's vengeful smile stained with Sophia's blood glared back at me. I angrily swung a fist across the stranger's pale face.

"What have you done to her, you fucking bastard? I'll kill you if you've hurt her! I'll kill you!"

The figure regained his strength quickly. He threw himself against me, pinning me against the wall of the passage, and suddenly stomped a hand against my chest. I froze as I felt a twisting pain crawl all over my body. The stranger's hand clawed at my chest, drawing blood. My shirt became soaked as the stranger's long nails ripped into my flesh.

"Not this time. Not again."

I screamed, trying to fight him off, but the stranger's strength was incredible.

Suddenly, a hand whipped the air across the being's face with the same powerful strength. The monster was flung back to the opposite side of the passage.

But he immediately rose, dusting off the webs from his black cloak. Ramiel was already breathing down his face.

"You!"

"What? Can't you say my name?" the intruder shrieked; then, he mumbled a phrase, the walls rumbled, and Ramiel stepped back, covering his ears.

I crawled to my feet and lifted myself from the ground beside Sophia's unconscious figure. I clenched my chest, looking down at the blood on my fingers. Sophia stirred; barely awake, she opened her eyes and glanced in my direction. I bent forward over her and pressed my lips over hers. Her warm mouth opened, and I pressed closer against her, caressing her breast. I could smell and taste the wine on her sweet lips.

"Amael..." she moaned softly as I pulled away from her. The stranger's laughter erupted from behind me.

I lifted Sophia in my arms, and she wrapped her arms around my shoulder, resting her face against my neck.

"Take Sophia out of here, Seth!" Ramiel ordered.

"No!" The figure screamed, edging towards me; but Ramiel caught him by the throat. Amael fought himself free and threw himself against Ramiel.

I obeyed the order given, and raced down the passageway with Sophia in my arms. She was barely conscious as we escaped through the corridor's exit and into the antechamber. The bouncers immediately came to my side scattering through patrons. I pushed through them as they stumbled to help me.

I rushed up the grand staircase into my office to lay Sophia on the table, which was still set up in my office from the meeting earlier. I leaned over Sophia concerned for her well-being. I would not lose her.

21

RESIN

RAMIEL

"You can't stop me."

"Poison, that's what you've become. An abomination of your own creation," Ramiel hissed.

Amael growled eerily, and dashed through the arched window with Ramiel in his grasp, launching them both into the sky. The two fought in the air, many feet from the ground below.

"Stay out of my way!"

"I can't!" Ramiel roared.

"Have you've forgotten who I am, Ramiel? Let me quickly remind you!"

At once, Amael swung his arm over; an arched fingernail sliced Ramiel's throat. Ramiel grabbed at his neck as Amael flung him down to the ground like a rag doll. Ramiel hit the side of the Cathedral back first, landing against the sharp peaks of the smaller towers. He groaned, painfully pulling at the peaks, fighting to jerk himself free from the structure, but losing his grip. He dangled helplessly, held in place and suspended over the street below.

His body bent over backwards. The pain was excruciating, but he had felt worse than this. Again, he struggled, pulling himself carefully free, feeling the skin and flesh tearing inside as he moved the spike from inside him. Too weak, he fell to the ground, unable to stop himself, and onto the roof of a parked vehicle down below. In a roaring crash, his body hit the top of the car and shattered its window shield. The whole incident had taken too much from him, and he lay motionless on the vehicle's roof.

A crowd gathered around the car; whispers spread among the curious spectators, evincing grave doubts that he was still alive. Someone yelled in the distance, "Call 911!"

But no one seemed to move. The bouncers rushed to the car as the sirens in the distance grew louder.

Slowly, Ramiel opened his eyes. He didn't sit up right away; aware he had been seen by a thousand spectators. The bouncers moved the crowd back.

Ramiel sat up; gasps of disbelief rose from some of the spectators standing in the distance. He climbed down the roof of the car; stumbling slightly at first, he quickly regained his balance. Ralph immediately raced to his side, but it seemed Ramiel needed no help. He pushed his way from them, unhurt.

Though there was a large bloody hole ripped through his jacket, he moved without trouble. Covered in blood, he glanced about, looking for Amael, before he tended to his wounds. However, there was no sign of him. The sky was dark and clear, with stars sparkling down at him.

"Should we call someone?" Ralph asked, examining his boss curiously with a perplexed look across his face. The other bouncers gathered behind him, examining the remains of the parked vehicle.

"No need for anything, gentlemen. Business as usual, no reason to get alarmed," Ramiel reassured them, gingerly dusting the remains of his jacket and addressing his audience.

"It's alright, everyone. I'm just fine, as you can see. That was just a reckless stunt. I hope nobody was frightened by it."

The crowd hesitated, and then finally gave Ramiel a round of applause. The bouncers kept looking up at the sky, wondering how he had pulled the stunt off.

"Mr. DeStefano, how did you do that?" Ralph, the head of security, asked with a quizzical look upon his face.

"Now, Ralph, I can't tell you that. If I tell you, I'm gonna have to kill you."

Ralph gave a hesitated smile, but the look on the owner's face seemed very much serious.

Ramiel walked back into the Cathedral, and glanced down at the large hole in his suit. He pulled apart the fabric and examined his gaping flesh; the huge hole in his stomach began to close, finally disappearing, as if it had never been there.

"Bastard ruined my suit," Ramiel uttered; even when in trouble, he still had his sense of humor. He'd need it, considering what was eventually going to occur.

22

I PUT A SPELL ON YOU

SETH

Man is a selfish creature. Everything in life is a selfish act. Man is not concerned with helping others, yet he wants others to believe he is.

"Sophia? Wake up! Are you alright?" Ramiel cried, lifting Sophia tenderly.

"Amael?" Sophia mumbled, opening her eyes; then she gazed up at Ramiel before she fell unconscious again.

Ramiel slammed his fist on the table. He noticed the wound on her neck was gone; just like his own wounds, they had vanished. But the harm had been done, and that's what he feared.

"What does she mean, 'Amael'?" I uneasily asked. A stir of worry fluttered deep in my gut. I leaned against the side of the table and reached over to tenderly touch Sophia's face. The idea of what could have happened if I hadn't come along looking for her was something I didn't want to consider it. That bastard had gone too far attacking her. I wasn't even sure what he had done to her.

"She means the DevilGod," Ramiel mumbled under his breath, removing his jacket.

His shirt was torn to pieces, so he pulled on a new, black, collarless shirt Ralph had brought into the office minutes after the battle.

He moved over to my side and instructed me to remove my own coat. I did as he asked and unbuttoned my bloodstained shirt.

"Let's have a look at those wounds."

"DevilGod?" I spoke the name Sophia had mumbled, pulling up the shirt as Ramiel bent over to examine the cuts on my bare chest. Ramiel nodded, placing his hand over each individual wound. I closed my eyes. I could still feel the pain as the intruder's claws pressed against my flesh.

"Relax, this won't hurt a bit," Ramiel sighed, noticing the expression on my face.

"How do you explain his uncanny resemblance to me?" I asked, opening my eyes and looking straight into the white-haired owner's gray ones.

"It's a trick," Ramiel was quick to answer, saying nothing more.

I didn't like it, but I tried to accept his answer. It made him nervous to think an evil thing like what I'd encountered could look like me, in any way. I hadn't noticed any familiarly to the thing before, and I knew it had not looked like that days ago. Was it changing in order to resemble me each time we met? If so, why?

"Forget about it," Ramiel softly hissed, obviously reading my thoughts.

"Well, what the hell is it? What happened out there, Ramiel? That bastard did something to her. Didn't he?"

"She'll be okay. He's stronger than I thought, though, too soon. That's the only thing that makes me nervous."

"What does that mean? Can't you stop him?" I nervously asked examining the expression on his face. If he was worried it troubled me far more.

"Of course, I can," he blankly mumbled, glancing back.

Ramiel moved his hand away from my chest and backed off to

give me room. Stepping away from the table, I examined my chest in a decorative mirror by the shelf. I was dumbfounded with the way the wounds had slowly sealed until they had completely vanished.

"How did you do that?" I breathlessly asked, shocked. "Is this some kind of illusion? It can't be. The pain is gone. Did you heal me? How?"

Ramiel didn't say a word as stepped over to Sophia.

"You have to stay alive, and keep your strength up. Right now, you have the upper hand. Amael has no body. Well, at least not a good body to sustain his existence, but that doesn't mean he can't kill you."

"Not if I kill him first," I was quick to answer, still trying to make sense of what had recently occurred. I touched my bare chest, trying to find the wounds any way I could, doubting whether they had really vanished, as I had seen them do.

"Don't be stupid, Seth. He can hurt you, even kill you."

"He won't touch me as long as you protect me, right?" I asked.

He hesitated momentarily, and it worried me that he had to think about it before answering. He blinked back. "That might be so, but he's powerful and growing stronger by the minute. I don't know how long I can protect you. You must stay close to me."

Again, Sophia stirred. I quickly leaned over and kissed her lips as Ramiel watched me with a vacant stare. I curiously gazed back at Ramiel, "What's wrong?"

"Nothing," Ramiel answered, putting his hand on my shoulder. "It's just I haven't noticed before how perfect you two look together. It reminds me of the first time I saw you both." Ramiel became silent, unable to avoid the questions of the past in my thoughts and eyes.

"What happened? Why did I lose her?" I asked gravely, struggling to find the answers on my own.

Ramiel looked back, his face bore a history I could only wonder about, a worry and pain I could only assume haunted his ghostly face. Even something such as that had never diminished his heart, no matter what had transpired. He had lived in a time beyond this, seen things I could only imagine. Sophia had always saw the stories he told me as he tucked me into bed as just that, mere stories and fantasies, but I knew better. He was preparing me for this very moment. He smiled as though he could see into my thoughts. The question was, was I ready for all this?

"Yes," he answered. "you are far more than ready. "You will remember with time, my friend, on your own. You've come a long way from that timid boy." Ramiel stared over at me, my memory hadn't returned completely. "I know she loves you, and you two belong together. Of that I can assure you."

I dropped my head sadly and walked to the door. "I only wish Sophia would believe that. I wish she loved me as I love her."

"She will come around, Seth. It's hard to accept, because you're her son. That's the wicked disguise. A method of confusion Amael has used to pervert the truth of your great love for each other. But we'll make her come to understand. Won't we?"

"I'd die for her," I declared softly, looking back at Sophia's figure on the table.

"I know," Ramiel whispered as a small grin appeared across his wrinkled face.

I examined Sophia, desiring her even as I stood only a step or two away. I could feel my heart beating uncontrollably. My emotions began to stir, and I could feel the lump of my arousal pushing through the fabric of my trousers. I wanted to feel her soft body against mine. The taste of her was still in my mouth; I wanted to force her to accept me. She would have no choice; the shame would be so great that she would have to love me. Once Nathan discovered the truth, she would have no choice.

I was sure Ramiel was aware of those thoughts as well as my desires within those moments. "You have to give her time. Don't push it. Don't force this upon her. She needs time."

"I want her by my side," I uttered again. I wanted to justify my actions to Ramiel, who I noticed was keen to every single thought coursing through my mind. "But the feelings were too strong. I feel shame almost for admitting this," I continued.

"What are you talking about, Seth?"

"I'm saying I forced myself upon her," I confessed angrily. Although I already suspected he knew this. Of course, he knew.

He didn't seem surprised, but was definitely disappointed. He took a breath moving around the office like a man on fire.

"That night, when he came. He stopped me. If he hadn't..." I continued, he spun back to face me, his face filled with rage.

Sophia began to stir at the loud sound of my voice.

"That was you." He said but its wasn't a question. I suspected he knew. "You attacked her."

"I wanted her. And he stopped me." I paused; I thought about that night again. Remembering the heated look of raw anger on the figure's face. The way the nostrils flared, and the eyebrows curved wickedly over his oval, white, evil eyes. Eyes that were glowing with white light, dancing with malice and eagerness and with some great urgency flowing from them. I wasn't looking at my own face, but one nearly and neatly identical to it. He far more divine, mature and wise, with a beauty even lovelier.

"He was afraid. I threw him out the window, but the bastard didn't die!"

"Seth..."

I glared back at Ramiel wickedly; the thoughts of that night were still running up and down my mind like the scratches on a spinning record.

"Why are you surprised?" I hissed, walking past him over to Sophia, who was lying on the table.

I touched her cold face with my warm hand, and kissed her. Again, I began to drift. My feelings were getting harder to resist as the scent of her perfume glided into my nostrils. I would have made love to her that very moment if Ramiel weren't there to watch me kiss her open mouth.

"I tried to resist, sitting back and allowing that bastard to touch her. But how can I when she's rightfully mine? If she's mine, what difference does it make?" I snapped, pulling away from Sophia, and trying to fight my desires.

It was obviously hard for me as I struggled to face Ramiel, who was bent over the table. I balanced myself, taking a deep breath, and then looked up. The desire was glowing on my face; every breath seemed my last.

Ramiel could see the heaving in my chest, the parting of my lips, and the gasping of my breath as I panted and exhaled in musical delight.

"It makes a whole lot of difference! She must love you...willingly!" Ramiel snapped, storming to the window.

"You mean, give in?" I beamed my black eyes straight at him, licking my mouth hungrily as the words left my dryly blistered lips.

Ramiel turned back around, his eyes disappeared beneath his thick eyebrows as he frowned. His wise and wrinkled face smoothed out, and suddenly became blank.

"No, she must accept you. Only then can she be yours," he hissed, letting his pointy canines emerge from behind the curve of his lips.

I rushed at Ramiel to face his already enormous height angrily. "Don't raise your voice at me. I'm not a child. Remember to whom you're talking!"

"Seth, I'm not your enemy. I'm trying to help you. Didn't you see the look on her face? She was terrified. Don't you care that you scared her?" Ramiel answered in a calm tone.

"Of course, I care!" I scolded and backed away, wandering to Sophia's side again, caressing her soft cheek.

"She's all I live for, but she hates me. How can I do anything without having her reject me? I hunger for her each day and night."

"You could have told me your plans before you acted on them."

"What for? So, you could lecture me as you are now? Perhaps rehearse some of your mystical mumbo jumbo? So far, your ways have miserably failed me."

"Have patience," Ramiel hissed, wrinkling a brow.

"There's no time for patience. Look at what happened today! Besides, I told Sophia the truth. That's what I did," I admitted, he didn't seem prepared for that news from the expression on his face. A smile beamed across my handsome face.

"You did what? Don't you see if you move too fast, you may lose her forever?"

"If I wait, I might lose her anyway. That bastard isn't playing fair. I won't lose her, not again," I hesitated, realizing my words and at the same time knowing that perhaps I had recalled some of the events of my past. But had the words seemed justified by Ramiel's own knowledge of the past, or my own recollection? I could not answer that.

"You remember?" Ramiel asked, his doubt seeming to slowly wither at the realization of my words. He gazed at me with a meager shred of excitement, yet my own expression seemed doubtful.

"I see only bits and pieces of something I used to know. She's there with me, and she loved me. The visions are only images of a long-forgotten past. The feelings are not."

"You can always count on your feelings. That is always your greatest power, Seth. Use it as I have taught you. Recall your greatest strength. It might be your only power now, but it's the greatest thing you can possess."

I fell silent and gazed down at my hands, as though something had been given to me by the words spoken so cautiously by Ramiel, who was older and supposedly wiser than me.

"Well, how did she take it?" Ramiel asked again, breaking the silence.

"How do you think?" I snapped, lowering my hands and crossing them. "She rejected me, of course." I furrowed my eyebrow slightly. "She despises me. I sicken her," I murmured again.

"What exactly did you tell her?" Ramiel asked, hovering closely to me.

I knew Ramiel had always considered me something of a student. I could sense it the way he cared and catered to my needs. But the studies here were not math, languages, the sciences, or anything like the classes in human schools. Though they were historical in a way, it was nothing like what teachers in regular classes taught their students. No, this was deep magic; this was the knowledge, the key to the throne of the greatest kingdom in the universe. And Ramiel felt privileged to teach me everything that he knew.

Although it nearly broke them, it was nevertheless within the rules of the realm that I would succeed. I would have the upper hand.

"I told her that we were meant to be together," I whispered softly.

"Why did you tell her that?"

"Isn't it the truth?" I remarked, flaring my eyes at Ramiel as he bit down on his lip. "But he wants to stop me. They both do," I said again, under my breath.

"Who else do you mean?"

"Nathan! My bastard of a father. The illusion of a father set up to stop me. He's standing in my way. Sophia loves him more than she loves me. I can't compete with him. We must get rid of him. He'll return soon. My chance to pursue Sophia will be ruined if he's around to interfere."

I took hold of Ramiel by the shoulders, hoping to appeal to his caring and nurturing side. I knew Ramiel would have an answer, although I felt like a child under the protective hands of my master. I didn't care, if it would help get the job done. I would pretend to be naïve, just this once. I would even betray the man who had fathered me; there was no doubt about it. I smiled as I rested my head on Ramiel's shoulder.

"Don't worry; I shall take care of everything, including Nathan. I will not fail you, my dear young friend."

Ramiel put his hand over my head and pressed me close. It seemed my warmth and attempts to be close and seek his approval delighted him, as well as gave him a sense of acceptance. It seemed to be the best reward he had ever received.

I smiled delightfully. Oh, how I hated Nathan; though despised was probably the better word. I couldn't wait to tell him how much. I wanted to see the look on his face when I told him I was in charge now; I would be running things, and he was no longer welcome. I owned everything, including Sophia's heart. And Nathan couldn't have her. I wanted to tell him everything of what I felt, what I was. The time would come soon enough.

"I'd better take Sophia upstairs to her bedroom. I'll be there, preparing the room," Ramiel said, pushing me gently away. He caressed a hand upon my cheek softly. He had always been like a father to me.

I nodded; recalling that the repairs in Sophia's room had been finished, and his only concern had been how to get her to return to it before Nathan returned. After today, that could be now more easily accomplished.

"What about those vampire fools? What if they start asking questions?"

"What about them? They didn't see anything. I wouldn't worry about them, Seth," Ramiel smirked cajolery as he lifted Sophia's body; she curled against him, mumbling.

"Perhaps you're right," I said, pushing the nest of black strands of hair from my face.

"They're harmless. Trust me. Now, you'd better change, before someone sees you and before Nathan returns," Ramiel said, walking out of the office with Sophia in his arms.

I nodded, grinning while removing the bloody shirt. I stood holding the bloody cloth in my hands, snickering wickedly as Ramiel vanished upstairs. A chuckle pressed through my lips and I began to laugh more freely. I finally fell over and slammed a fist on the table. Sophia would be with me finally. She would come to accept me; I had no doubt. And Nathan would know.

23

VAMPIRE LIQUID

L ucas kneeled near the toilet and threw up. A knock came from the other end of the stall.

"Are you alright in there, man? Want us to call someone?"

"I'm fine! *Go away!*" Lucas yelled back; the voice on the other side disappeared, and he didn't hear anyone again.

It was silent in there, and only the sounds of flushing and the faded music outside continued. Lucas felt fragile and helpless. He rose to his feet, but couldn't balance himself, so he fell on his knees again, gripping the toilet and dropping his face inside. The sour taste had returned; the liquid running down the side of his lip was clearly blood. He wiped it with his tongue, but it didn't taste the same, and the idea made him sick.

He was able to lift himself and push open the bathroom door. What had happened? He couldn't think clearly; he couldn't remember how he had ended up in the bathroom, bent over with his face in the toilet. Was it the vampire again? *Vampire,* he realized how foolish that sounded. There's no such thing as vampires. But now he wasn't sure any longer.

He didn't even know how long he had been gone this time, nor just how he had left the side of the bar, where he'd been. Only then did he realize exactly where he was. He pulled himself to the sink and rinsed his face and hands, desperately trying to recall the events that had led to this incident. However, his mind was completely blank.

He looked himself over in the mirror, staring into the pale features of his face. He looked wasted, drained, and tired. He hadn't slept in days; he couldn't remember the last time he had. But every time he blacked out, it seemed to make up for the lost sleep. And oddly, he felt well-rested, except for the sour taste he had acquired during his absence.

He bent over the sink to wash his face, then gazed back at his reflection, only now behind him he saw another reflection in the mirror beside his own.

He spun around as the white-haired intruder boldly stepped up to him.

Lucas' lips trembled as he noticed the figure's lips stained in blood smiling over at him, revealing a pair of double canines from the folds of his mouth.

"Soon, very soon!" the intruder hissed, grinning. Then, in a gasp, the image faded.

Lucas felt a gentle shove and fell against the sink; he took a breath as the image passed through him and vanished. Lucas dropped to his knees, at first unable to breathe, then exhaled desperately as if unseen hands had released his throat, allowing him a solitary breath.

"Soon, very soon." he repeated the phrase, invoked by a voice inside him.

He fought for control over his words, but the pain was stronger than anything he had ever felt. Instead, he screamed as yet another phrase forced its way through his quivering lips.

"Nathan, it is *complete*."

24

NATHAN'S UNWELCOME RETURN

RALPH

If a Wrong is gotten away with, and someone else repeats it and also gets away with it, is a Right birthed into existence?

I opened the door of the Lincoln as Nathan stepped out and greeted me with a shy smile. I had always liked the senior Abuda, because he was so kind and caring to every member of his staff. He treated us like a part of the family, and was civilized even when talking business with us. He was like an older version of Seth, but with a softer and more down-to-earth personality. Although the resemblance was keen, there were differences in many ways.

Nathan had a warm and caring smile unlike his son, who was mostly fake and devilish in his own twisted way. They both were well-dressed men, handsome and well-respected. The senior Abuda was kindhearted, and understanding in a style that I couldn't explain, like an innocence he had never truly lost. Mr. Abuda was quite unique, and I couldn't find myself disliking him in any way.

"Welcome back, Mr. Abuda."

Nathan appeared distracted, but flashed me a smile in greeting.

An uncertainty seemed to consume his gentle face as he looked up at the Cathedral he had always called home.

"Is something wrong, sir?"

"I'm not sure, Ralph. Where is everyone?"

"What do you mean, sir?" I asked, although I was certain what Nathan meant. Most night this is how things were, quiet. Although this evening, Seth and Ramiel seemed to be busy discussing business before I had left for the airport. It was strange to see Mr. Desfanto here for so long. He never extended his stays this long.

Had Nathan discovered what took place while he was gone? I wondered.

"The incident," as it had come to be known by my fellow workers was something I wasn't allowed to talk about.

25

DREADFUL TRUTH

NATHAN

I didn't say anything as I began to climb up towards the entrance of the Cathedral. Ralph unloaded my luggage from the trunk of the Lincoln.

Why hadn't anyone come out to greet me? Didn't they know I was returning today? I had called and spoken to Seth about my early arrival. The Lincoln had been sent for me, yet no one had come down the concrete steps of the monstrous Cathedral, not even my beloved Sophia.

An eerie feeling crept up and raced up my neck. I looked up at the towers and the Cathedral's peaks; its walls seemed to have a new aspect, different than usual. There was a strange sensation I now felt, like I was being watched, but the feeling soon left me, and I tried not to think about it as I made my way to the door and pried it open.

Inside, the same feeling aroused my fears. The same sensation that someone was watching me returned, and I found the antechamber of the Cathedral almost foreign to me. I couldn't explain why, but it grew as I walked deeper into the place that once had felt like home to me. I tried to think of Sophia. Her embrace would silence these unknown fears. I longed for her kiss, and her warm and caring smile. I could only think of her, and the uneasiness seemed be overpowered by thoughts of her. Now, I would be able to spend more time with her, take her away to foreign places as I had promised.

I pictured her standing at the foot of the staircase, looking down at me with a huge smile spread over her face. I hurried under the arch of the foyer. I could already see the grand staircase. My heart was throbbing as I raced forward, sensing her perfume through the air that brushed across my face. All I had longed for was my dear Sophia; every waking moment had been Hell in that hotel room. I had been a fool to have taken the job and abandoned my beloved, to let her fend for herself without me. I regretted it deeply, watching her cry when I left her side. I regretted the many nights I had spent without her in my arms, and felt jealousy for those that were rewarded with her precious presence. She was a constant delight of the heart, a continuous sparkle of eternal life. Why had I left? Why had I listened to countless others?

All I wanted was to be with Sophia, to spend my entire waking life with her, moment by moment in her divine presence. A single kiss wasn't enough; a single embrace and the clinging scent of her perfume wasn't enough.

I decided I would not leave again. I would abandon my duties and simply be with her. I could no longer be kept away. Ramiel would have to accept my decision.

I closed my eyes recalling Ramiel's words. "This is a good offer for you, Nathan. Make Sophia proud of you," Ramiel had casually remarked to me.

"Please, Nathan," Sophia said desperately on the phone, trying to hold back the tears. "Forget this. Please, come back. You don't have to do anything. We already have everything we need, right here."

"But Sophia, I want to give you everything without the help of any other; I want to be the one to make you happy."

"You have. Can't you see all I want, is *you?* Please, come back. I'm so alone without you."

I quickly realized my error. I had been selfish when all she wanted was to be with me. Nothing else mattered, not the money, only happiness.

But still, I had left that evening. Ramiel had handed me the plane ticket. I felt almost willed to take it, to use it.

It almost felt like Ramiel was trying to get rid of me, but it was ridiculous to think such a cruel thing. Ramiel had taken care of me after my accident many years back. He had brought Sophia and me together. He had given us this gorgeous place to live, and had been like a father to both of us.

In fact, my whole life had almost been a fantasy and a dream. I had a gorgeous wife, a beautiful place to live throughout my aging years, a prospering business and an intelligent and handsome son who could help run it.

I couldn't complain, but I'd been foolish to leave her behind. Yet, I couldn't help but wonder about Ramiel's intentions. It always seemed that he was the force drawing us apart. I didn't want to believe that.

"I don't want to leave Sophia alone," I pleaded on my last night at the Cathedral.

"She'll love it. You'll make her proud. She thinks it's a good idea," Ramiel had insisted, pushing me on my way out. Ramiel didn't know Sophia as well as he thought he did. I knew that much.

I'd said my good-byes and had taken the plane that evening to New York. I'd been in my hotel room late that night. As I lay on the bed, I'd held out a picture of Sophia, remembering the day it had been taken. It was a family picture.

I had an arm around Sophia. Little Seth, who was six at the time, sat by his mother's knee. He looked mature even as a child. I had always found it odd that a child so young had such adult expressions.

In another picture, I held him, but he seemed to be fighting my embrace. I'd never thought much about it then, perhaps excusing the fact that most children hated their parents hugging and kissing them.

Understandable. But now it troubled me, because I didn't have a good relationship with my son. This picture proved it.

I looked at a recent picture of us both, Seth standing alongside me outside the Cathedral. Seth had his arms crossed as he gave the camera a minuscule frown. He was dressed in an Armani black suit and a red tie. I stood beside Seth, with a hand resting on his shoulder.

Sinister looking lad, clever and threatening, were my first thoughts regarding the expression on his face.

I placed the picture back into the wallet, but kept Sophia's on the coffee table next to the bed. I lay back with the picture against the lamp, facing the bed, turning sideways to admire it. Then, finally, I closed my eyes.

Now, I was home once again. From my memories she materialized, even as I had seen her in my feverish mind. I froze and glanced up, but only a shadowy image beckoned me from the foot of the grand staircase.

Again, I wondered where everyone was. Had Seth forgotten me? No, I believed in Seth. Even though we had never been close, I trusted him. I only blamed myself for our emotional distance. Maybe if I'd spent more time with him when he was young, instead of allowing Ramiel to do so, things would be different. I should've rejected Ramiel's offer to tutor Seth, and take up my responsibility as a father. But I didn't blame Ramiel. I didn't resent him either. I would make up for my failures as a father and a husband. I was determined to do this.

I stepped closer. The shadowy figure was clearly visible, it was Seth. I waved, but he didn't acknowledge me nor smile. He strolled the upstairs oval-shaped office and disappeared. Had he not seen me? Or did he want me to follow? I didn't think much of it, for Seth had always been a strange child, quiet and withdrawn, closer to his mother than to me.

Nevertheless, I slowly climbed the flight of stairs, edging carefully to the top, mere inches from the entrance of the oval-shaped office. Once at the top, I stood at the entrance looking inside, and spotted Ramiel at the other end of the room examining a picture frame by the desk. Seth was standing facing the mirrored glass windows of the office, looking out into the dance dome.

I hesitated at first, then entered nervously, feeling the creepy uneasiness once again crawl up my neck. I was worried for Sophia. I wondered where she was, and why she wasn't here now.

I wanted to go in search of her, but I was rooted to the spot. I pressed my lips together and took another step forward. My mouth dropped.

"Ramiel? What's...going *on*? Is everything alright? Where's everyone? Where is Sophia?"

Ramiel slowly turned and greeted me with a smile, placing the frame back on the desk. For some reason, Ramiel's smile made me uneasy. I couldn't get rid of the feeling.

"Ah, Nathan, what a delight! Welcome home! You must forgive the lack of company! The children... you know them...they're out. They must have forgotten you were to arrive today. You did give us late notice," Ramiel said taking a few steps towards me. There was something off about his smile. I sensed the B.S. in his tone, but I didn't want to voice it. We had our moments where arguments became far more frequent, and I didn't have the patience this evening for such a disagreement.

"And Sophia—Where is she?" I asked. The vamps I could understand forgetting, but not my wife. I couldn't picture it.

"Sophia's asleep in her bedroom. She must have dozed off waiting for you..." I seriously doubted his words and they disturbed me. Why was Sophia back in her bedroom? She wouldn't willingly return to that place.

I was concerned she would so easily fall simply asleep knowing I was to arrive. Something didn't feel right; *they* didn't seem right in that moment. All I wanted to do was see my wife and head to bed. I was tired of this lifestyle and tired of missing precious moments with my darling wife.

Seth seemed different, his lips curved into a taught sneer, and he seemed almost to laugh at me. I felt my skin crawl.

There was something disturbing about the both of them. Something had changed, something was different, and it frightened me. Their eyes felt like invisible hands wrapping around my throat, trying to squeeze the last breath from me.

"Her *bedroom?* But why, I don't understand I thought...we'd agreed to...she would remain in the vaults at least until I returned?"

Ramiel was silent as he shrugged his shoulders.

I observed them. There was a deadly silence as Seth flashed me a dry smile. Ramiel broke the stillness between them. The gangly owner came closer, slowly encircling me. He was quite intimidating with his piercing eyes and ghostly locks of shoulder-length hair. It was mostly his grey eyes that ripped through my soul whenever I looked into them. They didn't look like any normal eyes I had ever seen.

"If you're worried about her safety, she's fine, Nathan. Everything has been taken care of; you can be sure of that," Ramiel assured.

"What do you *mean?* Is there something going on?" It was time to ask the obvious.

There was a long pause, and no answer to my question. I wanted to escape to see Sophia. But I couldn't move no matter how the door beckoned.

"I'm tired, Ramiel. I shall go see her...it's been a long trip and I'd like to head to bed, if you don't mind." I said my words slowly falling into a whisper as I moved towards the door. I wanted to get out of there. Something was telling me I should.

Before I made it to the doorway, Seth came to block me. I gazed at him, perplexed, as he flashed me the exact same clever smile he had given the camera in the picture in my wallet.

"So soon, Father? I thought that we could talk. After all, it is not often that you and I...well... have we ever?" He grinned.

"No, we haven't..." I said, as his smile spread.

"Ah, isn't this lovely? Father and son...chatting." Ramiel said. I caught Seth's eyes wrinkle slightly at those words. I found that strange; it bothered him whenever anyone included those words together, father and son. He looked ill.

"Can we talk tomorrow, son? I'm quite tired I just want to see your mother and head to bed."

He didn't move. I felt the uneasiness once more as Ramiel closed in from behind. Seth sinisterly grinned at me, refusing to move.

"No, I'm afraid this can't wait until tomorrow, Nathan," Ramiel announced. I didn't want to turn as I sensed him near me.

"What's going on?"

A hand came to rest upon my shoulder making me spin around to face the tall figure of Ramiel.

"Relax, Nathan; everything is alright," Ramiel said again. "We just want to talk to you. It's the least you can do for the son you hardly see."

I turned and faced him, unable to escape. His words ripped into me and I knew that he knew it. I hadn't been there for the boy and now he was shoving that in my face.

"What *is* it?" I asked curiously. What could be so important that it couldn't wait until tomorrow? Whatever it was, he now had my attention.

"There's something we must discuss. It's been on my mind for some time."

I had known Ramiel for a long time, remembered him when he had been cruel. He had been the one that had found me. He had brought me to Sophia. And I wondered why he was now trying to separate us.

"Listen *carefully!*" Ramiel said; his gentle face had hardened, and the white soft hair that had once made him glow and appear innocent now seemed enhanced by a hate-ridden stare. His voice roared and lifted like a trumpet.

From behind, Seth slammed the door closed, startling me. I glanced back. Seth stood a step or two behind. Entrapped by their figures, I wasn't sure what to think.

"What is it Ramiel? Has something happened?"

"Your time has come to an end, Nathan, that's all..." Ramiel said, as if he had plucked the very thought from my mind. An end, I had seen the end once. I'd been taken from its hands and brought here.

A vision knocked me back; somewhere in the light, I heard the familiar sound of gunshots. Then, the combined scents of gunfire and death blew in the voice of the wind. I tasted the blood down the side of my mouth as I took a breath, then collapsed to the floor.

I gasped staring over at Ramiel, who fashioned a cruel smile.

"Have you *forgotten?*"

"*No.*" I whispered. The word slowly escaped my mouth as the blood had.

Pain exploded within me. I held myself together, tears fought to escape the pooling in my eyes, as I lay still and prone.

"I can make it more painful," Ramiel said.

"Why are you doing this? Please...Ramiel, stop! *Please...*What have I've done?"

I held a breath as the pain shot into my body again.

"You know this was always meant to be. You have served your purpose for the time. Now, you must step aside. You have a choice to voluntarily leave, or I can kill you. Make it easy on yourself."

"Please, *stop!* I did as you asked. I kept Sophia safe, I loved her. Why now?" I gasped and heaved as the pain rode down my stomach; it seized me, ebbing for a moment, but I knew it wasn't completely gone, and I knew the next time the pain would be twice as unbearable. Nonetheless, somehow, I staggered to my feet.

"If only you understood, Nathan, that you are only part of the solution. Only a half of what Sophia needs." I wrinkled my eyes over at him. What did he mean?

"And I need that part, that half of what you hold inside you to make Seth complete and whole once and for all."

I glanced over at Seth in desperation; turning slowly away from Ramiel, I hoped to leave, but there was no escape. I didn't understand any of what Ramiel was talking about, but I knew he wanted me dead. Seth flashed me a smile, slowly moving aside as I reached out to him, and then I collapsed to the floor, locked in the deepest agony again.

"Help me, son! Please, help me!" But he moved away. I couldn't believe he was allowing this. Did the boy hate me that much?

"This is the only way, Nathan. You think you would live a life that doesn't belong to you? The life you have is but borrowed...it was never yours to have, my dear Nathan."

Ramiel kneeled beside me. I lifted my head, barely meeting his eyes.

"None of this belongs to you, my dear boy. It was never meant to be for you. You were only getting things ready for the true lord." He pointed towards Seth, who beamed down over me. I couldn't tell if he was agreeing with this. He seemed reluctant in some form. "Even Sophia."

"No!" I gasped reaching out to him, but the boy wouldn't acknowledge me.

"Don't you *see*, my dear Nathan? The boy wants you dead more than *anyone*. With you out of the way, Sophia will now take her rightful place with Seth, where she was always meant to be."

I blinked quizzically. "But she's his mother," I stuttered

"The idea that she was his mother was your belief, poor Nathan. Sophia never had a child..."

"No...you lie. I saw him his birth...I saw." I ran the memories through my mind.

"You saw only what I wanted you to see, Nathan. This has always been your illusion, my poor Nathan, to get what I needed from you. And now, the time has come...no more illusions; no more games..."

"No! *No!* Why my Sophia?"

"She's not yours! She was *never* yours!" Seth yelled from the other end and rushed forward. He caught me off guard. He seemed just as surprised by his words. He froze, glaring at me angry. His nostrils heaved with a strange rage. What was wrong with him? He seemed like a different person suddenly, one that despised me and wanted me dead.

"Son? Seth?" I pleaded, reaching out to him, but he walked around me, ignoring me.

"You're not even my father. You're nothing. You're just a vessel. A tool used, and now, one to discard like a piece of trash!"

"Just step aside, Nathan," intoned Ramiel. "take your place, be a part of this. For you still can. You can live on within the boy. You can live comfortably as part of him."

What? Live within him? What did that mean? I had to save Sophia and get her out of this wicked place. All this made no sense.

"No, damn you! No! I love Sophia! I can't be without her. I won't leave her! Ramiel, this is crazy!"

The pain faded again. I struggled to my feet and turned to face Ramiel and Seth, who were both standing before me. Seth's laughter roared and bounced off the walls of the small office as he loomed upon me, his wicked smile bearing down.

"She's mine. She will love me. This is the way it should have been. We've been kept apart for far too long."

"NO!" I screamed, rising and shoving Seth back, I swung a fist at him. Seth's head tossed back as my hand knocked the side of his lower jaw. His hand reached over wiping at the scarlet stain upon his lip.

I backed away unto the doorway; my hands shaking.

"I *won't* let you touch her. I won't let either one of you hurt her!" I yelled, grabbing for the doorknob. "We are *leaving* this wretched place!"

Flinging the door open, I raced out of the office, up to the second level corridor.

26

THE MAN OF YOUR DREAMS

SETH

I moved to follow him, but a tug from Ramiel stopped me.

"Let him go."

"But he'll tell Sophia *everything*. We must stop him!"

"He won't do anything. I know him well. Besides, Sophia won't remember the events of last night or this night well enough to believe him," Ramiel said. That assured me.

"What will we do with him?" I asked, feeling over the side of my throbbing jaw and licking the blood from my mouth.

"Kill him," Ramiel very boldly said. He seemed stern, like a very emotionless fiend. "I'm afraid I can't," Referring to himself.

"It'll be my *pleasure*." I said smiling back. "That subhuman bastard is as good as dead, as of today."

27

RUDE AWAKENING

ERIC

Magic is like a combination lock. If each tumbler falls into place, the lock will open.

I hid as Nathan raced up the staircase past me. I still couldn't believe what had taken place downstairs in the oval office between Nathan, Ramiel, and Seth, his son. The incident was fresh in my mind, and I couldn't make sense of it. I wanted to believe I was dreaming, perhaps imagining the whole thing. It would be less troubling. However, I couldn't pretend any longer that I hadn't sensed something strange in Seth's actions toward Sophia. I had never suspected Ramiel to be any part of this, though. Now, I was afraid.

Confused, but most of all disappointed, all my beliefs seemed to diminish within those few seconds. I was concerned for the safety of Sophia and Nathan. What did all this mean? But more importantly, what did it mean for Sophia and the rest of us?

I had to warn Sophia. We had to leave, like Nathan had declared, before things got worse. We couldn't stay another day in this place!

I feared the worst. Had Ramiel and Seth been planning this from the very beginning? All these questions, with no answers.

I began to weep; and couldn't stop myself. Things had been wonderful once; now, they seemed to be falling apart thread by thread. The events of this fateful day rolled from my mind like a floating standard of warning. Earlier, Ramiel encouraged us, even invited us to go shopping, while he and Seth remained back at the Cathedral. Ramiel arranged everything; dropping us off at the Galleria shopping center, and leaving us without a method of transportation home. We were to call whenever we were ready.

But restlessness had set in my heart as soon as we had arrived. The others did their shopping, but I couldn't brush the morbid thoughts from my mind. Finally, feeling defeated by the uneasiness that had plagued me, I dismissed myself from my companions, complaining of not feeling well. I took a taxi back home. I hadn't felt good the whole afternoon. I'd worried I had caught something from our new bartender. After all, the guy had been sick the entire evening. Angelo told me Lucas had been in the bathroom, throwing up most of the day. But then, Angelo had served him several shots before he allowed the new guy a go at the bar. That was Angelo's steadfast rule.

"Can't touch the stuff, if you can't take a shot!" However, it had been several, and after a while, anyone- even an ardent vampire- would have been sick.

I struggled to my feet; carefully stepping over the rails, and ducked under the arch, hoping to pass the office unseen and head toward the vaults. However, as soon as I began to descend, a shadowy shape cast itself upon the walls of the Cathedral, heading in my direction. I backed away and scampered back into the spot where I had hid when Nathan had hurried past me. Who was coming?

I waited nervously, but no one appeared. The shadow seemed to disappear into the darkness of the building. Only the silence surfaced to mock me, a rush of wind hit my face. Paralyzed, I remained where I was, looking ahead. The shadow reappeared rising from out of the floor. A three-dimensional form shaped itself from out of a black cloud taking on a human form without a face. It was completely black, and that scared me.

The shape transformed further, slowly resembling the appearance of a human. I could see a face now take shape; eyes and lips seemed to surface from out of the blackness. White, long hair devoured the black shell and a man now stood before me. He was a handsome man dressed in a red velvet vest and long silk cloak with beautiful glowing skin, and spectacularly white long hair. He was glowing so brightly that I blocked my eyes with a hand. The glow soon faded, and light hummed from the stranger instead.

I couldn't believe how alike in appearance to Seth's and Nathan's faces the stranger seemed to be. At first, I thought it was Seth or some kind of joke. But to my horror, it wasn't. I moved back, falling down. My scuffles drew the stranger's attention to me. He spotted me ducking in the corner of the passageway.

The figure gave me a smile, I shuddered as he took a step towards me, but stopped glancing away toward the end of the passageway. He seemed to be drawn away. He glanced at me once more lifting a pale finger and instructing me to be silent."Ssshhhhhhh!"

I heard steps coming from the other direction of the passageway and turned with mock courage to challenge the sounds. Who was coming now? I glanced back at the intruder, but the shadowy presence that had appeared had vanished.

Unable to make sense of what I had seen, I raced down the passageway and under the arch. I would have to escape the long way out of the Cathedral to avoid the other ghost. I wasn't going to wait and see.

28

AMAEL, BE THOU NAME

NATHAN

The hunter must hunt. The moment he stops, he becomes the hunted.

I entered Sophia's bedroom and closed the door behind me, locking it.

I felt pain crawling all over my body, inside and out. However, I had to be strong for Sophia and protect her from the reality of their world. I had to protect her from Ramiel and...Seth! A sob broken through my mouth; I held back, swallowed hard. I had to keep it together. The very idea of what they planned was sickening. How could all this be a fantasy of mine? I didn't believe it. But why then did I feel there was some truth to it? Had I really seen his birth; had I really bared a son? Did I want to believe Ramiel's lie for the mere idea of living this life that he claimed was not even mine. The people I trusted with my life had come to take me apart. Had I known it, and merely denied it? Had I sacrifice so much to live a lie?

Perhaps I had no choice, and was a vessel, as Ramiel had claimed.

A tool for their plans to plant the seed of evil? And Sophia, what was *she* to them? What was her role? The mysteries had always lain in her, from the moment I had discovered her. She was a mystery the first time Ramiel introduced her to me.

A woman without a past, without a family. All I knew was that I loved her. The past didn't matter and didn't scare me. I had all the answers then, but now I doubted my entire life. However, never Sophia; she was the only thing that made sense to me. I knew I loved her, and my great friend and master, Ramiel, was so protective of her from the beginning. I should have known, should have seen the evil he hid. But my love for her had blinded me from seeing anything past what I felt for her.

"Come in, Nathan," Ramiel's voice had whispered softly from inside the room. His tall figure was standing in the dark watching Sophia sleep soundlessly.

I recalled opening the door, poking my head into the room and stepping in quietly. I saw her shape on the bed near the lamp glowing dimly, next to the coffee table. Nervously, I pushed back black locks, trembling under the eyes of Ramiel.

The wounds had healed long ago. Yet, now, I couldn't stop thinking of the pain. What deal had I made? Had I made a pact with the devil? And if so, was it finally coming to an end? I didn't want to give it up. Not Sophia.

I gazed over momentarily up at the tall figure of Ramiel, then searched the covers of the bed for the being I loved long before I had set eyes on her.

"Is that the girl you told me about Master...*Sophia?*" I recalled asking, looking towards the bed where Sophia lay.

———

I CLEARED MY HEAD, holding my stomach. The pain had seized me, and I knew it wasn't gone. It was only a matter of time before it would come back and make me beg for my life. I walked over to the bed, finding Sophia lying underneath the covers. She still looked the same, like the first time I had set my eyes upon her. Like that night in the dark room, with Ramiel's figure standing over her, glaring down at me from the side of the bed. It had never occurred to me before how she hadn't changed, or aged a single day since we met. However, now as I looked at her, it puzzled me, yet made sense.

I stumbled to the side of the bed, balancing myself on the frame, then stopped and collapsed on the bed next to her. My weight shifted the bed slightly, and Sophia suddenly awoke.

Shaking the sleep from her eyes, she looked at me. A smile spread over her face, and her eyes sparkled to life as she sat up to embrace me.

I practically fell into her arms, holding her tightly taking her in. Sophia sensed there was something wrong.

"Nathan, you're here. Oh, how I missed you so much! I must have fallen asleep; when did you get in? I'm *so* glad to see you. I've *missed* you!" She seemed to have a million things to say. She kissed me passionately. I didn't want it to end.

Sophia held me, as I trembled in her arms. She gently pulled away and caressed my soft cheek, looking into my eyes. I pulled her to me, hoping to hide from her. I kissed her instead and tucked my face against her neck. I just wanted to be with her one more time, before she was ripped from my arms. Before I had to...

I stopped myself. I didn't want to think about it, and held her tightly in my arms.

"Nathan, what's wrong?" Sophia whispered gently.

However, I answered her with a kiss, pressing my lips on her soft mouth to make room for our reality.

Sophia fell back on the bed. I came over her. I could still feel the pain inside me, that part that warned me. *I'll be back!* However, I pushed everything away. Closed my mind to the pain and the faces of death that had once mocked me. This was our time together.

I pushed inside her, kissing the back of her neck tenderly. Immediately, her hands pressed me closer. Her warmth overwhelmed me, and I was lost in her embrace. She quivered beneath as we came together again and again.

"I love you, Sophia. I *always* have, and I always will."

"I know, Nathan, I love you, too," she answered in a whimper. A wave of energy shot through me, a feeling of complete peace and pleasure coursed like the blood flowing throughout my moving body.

"Sophia!" I quavered, biting at my lips.

The pain submerging inside me became one with the feeling, one with the pleasure.

"Yes, Nathan, that is the Lady Sophia," Ramiel's voice again said. The past returned to haunt me one more time.

"Remember what I told you?" Ramiel said.

"I don't believe it," I whispered. I couldn't believe how beautiful she was. I immediately fell.

"You must. It's your destiny," Ramiel angrily snapped back.

It's your destiny.

Had I ever accepted his destiny?

A passion of emotion shot within me and I felt the ecstasy overcome me. Sophia quivered beneath me, and after a while, she was silent. I kissed her neck, lying in her arms, unable to move. Sophia's naked body curled beside me, and she fell asleep in my arms.

For a moment, I lay listening to the silence perhaps wondering if Seth or Ramiel would enter and force me away. After a moment of waiting, nothing happened. The only thing I could hear was Sophia's breathing as she lay beside me. I couldn't sleep and rose instead, glancing back at Sophia before struggling across the room, half undressed. I pulled at the white robe from the closet door and stumbled into the small bathroom at the other end of the room. I had made up my mind. I would fight this. I would fight for Sophia. I would tell her and leave with her, tonight when no one was looking.

I'd asked the others to join us, perhaps Eric could make the necessary arrangements so we could all leave. We could sneak away with the money I had saved. I was no fool; I had planned my own escape for some time now fearing Ramiel's change in tone. I was glad I had listened to that inner voice.

We could use that to survive until we could get on our feet. It was more than enough. I would go to Europe, perhaps visit Paris. Perhaps the vamps had friends in the area. Eric had lived in London before, and wasn't Santiago originally from Spain? It didn't matter; we would go far away to protect Sophia from Ramiel and Seth. I knew the vamps would help me. We would hide out, change our names if we had to.

I grabbed at my stomach. The pain was unbearable. How much more could I endure? Doubt began to sink in. Could I truly escape this? Would I make it out alive? What control did Ramiel have over me?

I bent over the sink and splashed some cold water over my face, looking at my reflection in the mirror. I had to protect Sophia, that's all I knew. I had to save her from this disgusting situation, that's all that kept going through my mind.

This can't be right. None of it.

"You're not my father!" Then who was I? What was all this?

It was time to take action.

I lowered my head, gripping the sink, and then glanced in the bathroom mirror at Sophia's figure on the bed. She stirred, but didn't wake. How could I tell her the truth, that we had been brought together by a force that now wanted to pull us apart? I was a dead man waking up from a dream I couldn't let go of. A dream that wasn't mine. I couldn't believe it myself, but I knew it was true.

In fact, I believed we had been part of something much greater, something of which we had no real understanding. Something we had never been aware of, until now. However, I still couldn't completely understand. Perhaps there was no sense understanding it, no point now.

I looked at my reflection in the mirror and began to cry. My tears could not save her. I stared at my image. At a second glance, I saw a blur race across the mirror. I looked again, but found my own reflection staring back at me. I turned from the mirror to grab the towel on the rack, when I was confronted by a figure. The image of a man with long, white hair stood blocking my path. I stumbled back as the stranger stared right into my awestruck eyes. Who was he?

I heard the voice again as I felt the pain growing inside me. The stranger lifted a hand to my face and touched my forehead. Immediately, I felt light-headed. A swarm of voices yammered. It sounded like the wails and wheels on a carousal, along with screaming children running down streets storming inside my head. I saw an endless vision of a dark place expanding over the horizon. A realm was now revealed beckoning me forward.

Eerie music grew and became louder, and a shapelessly, distorted face showed me a place with old buildings once resembling large cities that now lay in ruins. On the horizon, an unseen band played a church organ melody; it was a theme that haunted the deserted roads and buildings of this spooky place. Just in the distance, there was a circus, strangely inviting, it looked like Hell had come alive.

Images of children playing and running into the circus and in the ruins of a playground materialized and disappeared into the dark cobwebbed tunnels of an oblique maze. Even their innocence was distorted. Beneath a rusted path of tiny holes- like hollow eyes sockets- and gaps revealed darkness and fire, suspended over an abyss. The carousel horses, once plastic were now made of wood. The fading paint had been eaten away by time.

Here, the rivers were made of waste; blood dripped from the bright red roses, and no birds perched on the branches of the dying, leafless trees. Large vultures and bats flew around in a darkly macabre overcast crimson sky.

29

THE APPLE HAS BEEN ROTTING

AMAEL

My name is Amael. I remembered, did he? I lifted my head, staring at the reflection of myself in the mirror. I touched my face, looking over my features in complete wonder. Had this been my face all along? There was a smile upon this face. How different it appeared, but this was me. I looked over at my hands; they had been foreign to me. I turned sideways, the grin on my face softened when I caught a sight of her figure upon the bed. I turned hurrying out, balancing on the walls when I lost my step, then on the frame of the bed.

Walking seemed to be new to me, foreign like the smile on my face, like these large black eyes and this thin, body. However, I managed to stumble to her side and took a seat on the bed. She was lovely, how I missed her... her touch, her scent, her warmth.

I reached over and touched her face; Sophia slowly opened her eyes and looked up at me with a smile. I bent over and kissed her, longing to touch her.

"Come to bed, Nathan. Hold me," she whispered, before closing her eyes.

She saw no one else but Nathan. She didn't know my true name.

I nodded and rose clumsily to remove the robe. But stopped, and for a moment watched her sleeping and wondered if she could feel me now better than before. She hadn't given me any indication this was true; perhaps it was too soon to tell. I had to wear the body, connect with the flesh. Then she would see me.

"I'm here," I whispered, but Sophia didn't move; she just lay still, fast asleep.

I felt like a fool. Had I hoped she'd jump in my arms, delight in my coming? I had hoped for a more romantic reunion.

It would not be easy. I wanted to wake her, explain to her who I was, but I knew that would be pointless. She had to see for herself. She had to feel me, come on me. She had to find me on her own. When she was ready, she would know. Until then, I would be here, waiting for her. Waiting and protecting her from the danger of which she was as yet unaware. Wasn't she?

I pulled the covers away, and then froze. Even in this body, some of my senses were familiar and I could still feel the presence of another, of my enemy.

I fastened the straps of the robe around my waist and moved towards the door, almost entranced by the sense of someone approaching. I glanced back at Sophia before I reached for the door-knob; then, I walked out into the open passageway, which was dark and deserted. I'd never feared the dark; it had always been my friend. I moved down the passage, feeling uneasy by the shadows and shapes cast by the lights at the other end.

I came to the end of the passage and looked down and over the rails, moving underneath the arch. I continued, now descending the stairs one-by-one. I could get used to this body; though it was small, I would manage. Its growth would follow in time, and I would change it to better suit me. However, I would wait until my being occupied every single space of the skin. Until it became attached, and it would with time.

I stopped at the end of the steps, still unable to find what I was looking for. My powers and abilities were easily lost in this new form.

With time, I would regain control. I continued down another flight of stairs; below was the oval office, the door of which laid wide open. I stopped at the bottom, took a step or two towards the entrance, and sneaked a look. No one was there; I was alone. I came closer, touched the wall, and examined the interior and its mirrored glass window. I moved away from the entrance, stepped over the edge of the grand staircase, and looked down at the bottom.

An unidentified presence seemed to hover nearby, close to me. Why couldn't I identify its source?

The presence seemed to vanish, and I examined the interior of the Cathedral for any signs of it, but I saw nothing, nor did I feel it. I wanted to return to Sophia. I would rather be with her and lose all my abilities than to be alone and powerful.

I moved away, but a cold breeze brushed the back of my neck, like a hand moving down behind my shoulder. It seemed to knock into me and shove me forward.

I spun around, trying to balance myself. I still hadn't gotten hold of the body's legs. Yet I moved, reaching out, I found Seth standing and blocking the path behind me.

The youth grabbed me by the collar, lifting me. We face each other. I was powerless, my body was like a porcelain doll in Seth's hands. I attempted to take flight, only to realize my human body would not allow me to escape.

"It's time to *die,* old man! Don't worry about Sophia—I'll take *good care* of her!"

Had he known? Did he know Nathan was inhabited by the figure that stood before him? I had saved Nathan the agony of this diminished and cruel death, yet as one, we would share the end together.

Seth shoved me with one quick push, letting me fall back. I tried to reach out, but failed to grip Seth's arm. I tumbled backwards, unable to hold onto anything, hitting the steps headfirst, cracking my skull at the first bounce. One-by-one, I bounced on each step, rolling back, snapping my collarbone in two places, and finally landing at the bottom of the stairs, where I couldn't move. Surely Nathan wouldn't have survived such a fall.

Upon the body of Nathan's last breath, I moved through it, aching to escape before death had me again. I streamed out of the mouth, and as Nathan's breath elapsed, I heard the last beat of the heart behind me, then it finally stopped, and this body was dead.

I saw Seth standing at the top of the staircase, slowly moving back, swallowed by the darkness, concealed in what he had once known. The shadows now protected him. I only saw his image one last time before I was forced to flee, defeated once again.

30

THE REALITY

SOPHIA

I opened my eyes and looked around the room, spotting a figure walking up to the bed. He kneeled along the side of the bed near me. I turned the light of the lamp on, and noticed it was Nathan. He seemed to be sobbing.

"Nathan, what's wrong?" I asked, sitting on the bed a few steps from him.

Nathan stared up at me with a difficult attempt of a smile on his face.

"I love you, Sophia. I always have. You know that," he began to say.

I didn't like the sound of his tone.

"Yes, of course I do," I said nervously.

"But I failed you. I let him come between us. I'm sorry..."

"Nathan, what do you mean? I don't understand. Who? No one's come between us. Please, tell me my love, I don't understand."

"I knew, and yet I did nothing. I couldn't, you see. I'm sorry. I thought you would have.... I thought you would have known.... But you didn't, and then *he* came. I don't want to lose you, but he took the chance from me."

Nathan dropped his face into his hands. I didn't understand who he was talking about. No one could ever take me away from him and I wanted him to know it. I dropped from the bed to his side and reached to touch him, but I couldn't feel him. It was as though he wasn't there. But he was; I could see him. I gasped, pulling back.

I wasn't scared; I didn't understand what was happening to him.

"Nathan?"

Nathan lifted his face and reached out to me. I moved to take his hand, but in that moment his image faded, and he was gone. All I could hear was his voice, softly and gently weeping and fading around me.

"Forgive me, Sophia."

"Nathan?"

I awakened and sat up on my bed. I'd been dreaming but why did it feel so real?

I looked around the room, and jumped out of the bed. Somehow, I felt doubtful. I rushed to the bathroom, throwing the door open and looked inside, but it was empty. I began to sob, doubt burned inside and grew.

"No, it couldn't be...*Nathan!*" I called out, looking here and there for signs of my husband. I feared the worst. I sensed it in my very core. I screamed and rushed to the door, and then raced down the passageway, hoping to see Nathan foolishly standing by the rails, looking back as he had many times before.

"Nathan!" I cried again; the walls echoed with my voice.

I couldn't stop crying; the feelings were overwhelming. All I wanted was to see him, to scold him for frightening me. I could feel his arms around me. I could see his smile penetrating the pale, smooth skin of his face. All I wanted was to hold him once more.

What could the dream mean? Had it been a dream? I couldn't be sure anymore. My dreams, my reality were growing into one unknown world. I didn't want to believe it, none of it. I didn't want to believe something bad had happened to Nathan. Yet, the feeling was there, and I couldn't shake it.

"Nathan, please be alright! *Please!*" I stumbled forward practically leaping down the flight of stairs to the second level, and swiftly stood steps away from the entrance of the oval office, staring in.

Flashes of Nathan's face, images of his times with me crept into my mind, twisting me so horribly I shook them away.

I stopped. His smile in my mind found me as well as the taste of his kiss on my mouth. His scent was on my hair.

"*Nathan!*" I screamed; my eyes bulged, my hands trembled, as a cry was torn from my lips again, twice as loud.

I dropped to my knees, spotting Nathan's body at the bottom of the grand staircase, lying still and in a spreading pool of blood.

"NOOOOOOOO!"

I rose with difficulty to my feet, balancing myself on the stair rails and hurried to the bottom. I kneeled by his side. I took his head in my arms and began to cradle him, hoping I could revive him, but as much as I wanted to deny it, I knew it was too late.

"Please, darling! Please, be all right!"

My cries brought the others to my side. The vamps found me by Nathan's side, weeping. Eric came over and kneeled beside me trying to pull me away. I resisted at first, then fell into his arms, a weeping mess. The others dropped to their knees, some sobbing, and some praying.

"This *can't be!*"

31

A DEATH IN THE FAMILY

ERIC

"Someone call an ambulance!" I pleaded, trying to be brave for Sophia.

No one moved at first.

"Go! Now! Get some help, damn it!"

Angelo and Damon scattered to their feet, racing to the oval office to make the call.

"Please, tell me he's not dead, Eric! Please, tell me he'll be okay!" she begged me.

However, I knew better and could do nothing else but shake my head, and hold her in my arms. I couldn't stop thinking of what I had heard. I had to tell Sophia about Nathan's confrontation with Seth and Ramiel. I wondered if they had something to do with Nathan's death.

I didn't want to think about it. However, the thought wouldn't leave my mind. I feared for Sophia, now more than ever.

I pulled Sophia to her feet, and away from Nathan's lifeless body. In the distance, I could hear the sirens drawing near. The place would be crawling with medics and perhaps a few policemen taking statements, then everyone would leave, and it would be quiet again, but it would not change anything.

Nathan would still be dead.

Sophia's eyes flickered before she lost consciousness and collapsed in my arms. I lifted Sophia; my lips touched her soft mouth when I cradled her close against my body, feeling her helpless in my embrace.

Santiago and Valentino jealously observed me, lifting their gazes off the floor away from the mangled body of Nathan. I could almost sense what they were thinking; Sophia was now completely alone, and utterly helpless.

Sophia's lips kissed my ear softly in a whisper; then she nestled close to me, wrapping her arms around me as she sobbed again.

"Will you stay with me, Eric?"

"I shall not leave your side, my dear."

Damien and Riccardo came to my side and followed me up the flight of stairs as I carried Sophia in my arms to the second floor and into the oval office. Entering, I lay her on the leather sofa. The Elders entered, along with the others. Damon and Angelo were near the desk. Angelo hung up the phone as I kneeled in front of Sophia.

"They're on their way."

"I wish they'd hurry!" Riccardo mumbled sadly and nestled near Damien.

Damien held Riccardo closely, ruffling the black hair on his head softly like a nurturing mother. Damon stepped over to his companion and put his arm around her and Riccardo, holding them closely.

"It's gonna all be fine," I tried to assure them, but I wasn't sure myself anymore.

Damien looked up at her companion, doubtfully, as she broke into silent sobbing. I rose, sighing and very much troubled at what I had to revealed.

"There something I must tell all of you. Something very important." Their eyes immediately stared over at me.

"What is it, Eric?"

Angelo stepped away from the phone, and the expression on his face turned into one of concern. Even the Elders took an interest in what I had to say.

They came closer, huddled in the center of the room where the others stood surrounding me and Sophia's body by the sofa.

"I heard them arguing just before Nathan's death. I heard them," I said quickly. their attention was completely on me.

"Heard *who* argue?" Angelo interrupted.

"I should have seen it coming," I said nervously, ignoring Angelo's question.

"What are you talking about, Eric?" Damon asked, wrinkling a brow, and then gazing at the others, who were just as confused as he.

"Yeah, tell us. We'd sure like to know," Santiago griped.

"Don't you *ever* shut up?" Angelo snapped back. "Let him *talk!*"

"Guys! Come on, have a little respect. Nathan is dead. For Sophia's sake, please!" Damon insisted angrily. He hugged his companion closely, and then stepped over to my side.

I moved to the window silently. I couldn't stop thinking about what I'd heard, and what had taken place the minute after. And what about the figure in the passage? Could he be responsible for Nathan's death?

I wasn't even sure.

"What is it, Eric? Is it about Nathan?"

"Yes..." I whispered softly, spellbound by the bitterest of circumstances.

Dear reader,

We hope you enjoyed reading *Existence*. Please take a moment to leave a review, even if it's a short one. Your opinion is important to us.

Discover more books by S.C. Lewis at https://www.nextchapter.pub/authors/cs-luis

Want to know when one of our books is free or discounted for Kindle? Join the newsletter at http://eepurl.com/bqqB3H

Best regards,

S.C. Lewis and the Next Chapter Team

You might also like:
Heir of Ashes by Jina S. Bazzar

To read the first chapter for free, head to:
https://www.nextchapter.pub/books/heir-of-ashes